Pieces of Me

Bri Kittrell

Kindle Direct Publishing

Copyright © 2024 Bri Kittrell

All rights reserved. First Edition.

The characters and events portrayed in this book are fictitious. Any similarity to real persons, living or dead, is coincidental and not intended by the author.

No part of this book may be reproduced, or stored in a retrieval system, or transmitted in any form or by any means, electronic, mechanical, photocopying, recording, or otherwise, without express written permission of the publisher.

Cover design by: Canva

To my husband and family, for always being the shining light that keeps the darkness away.

To my beautiful Archer and Isabelle, may you never question just how loved and treasured you are.

Content Warning:

This is a new adult romance with sexual content and language. This story contains heavy themes of depression, self-harm, death, addiction, grief, mentions of child abuse, and violence. Your mental health matters, so please take caution when reading.

Chapter One

Sam

Someone once told me that time has a way of balancing things, of righting the wrongs and giving back what was taken away. I don't know what genie lamp they rubbed in their lifetime to befall such luck, but all time has ever done is screw me over. I spent so much time as a child trying to be the perfect daughter and be just like my parents, but I always felt that when they looked at me, they were disappointed they couldn't see slivers of themselves.

My mother's rich auburn curls that smelled of lavender and rosemary were a stark contrast to my light blonde waves. Her meadow green eyes with flecks of gold held a warmth that my icy blue ones never could.

My father's honey-colored gaze and chocolate brown hair should have won out in the genetics department, but they instead created the anomaly that is me. I still tried every day, though, to learn their hobbies and goals so that I might succeed in them as well. I might not look like them, but perhaps I could be like them. I tried to learn Dad's recipes, and nearly burned the kitchen down a few times. I even spent hours in the garden watering

Mom's plants, checking the soil, and trimming the leaves just to have each plant I touched die.

All I ever wanted was to make my parents proud, especially my mom. I thought maybe I was close to connecting with her the way I always yearned for when she smiled at the garden of lavender and roses that I sketched her, but then cancer ravaged her body and ripped her away. She suffered for months, and I had to sit back and helplessly watch the light leave her eyes, and I fell deeper into the darkness that resides in my mind. She died and took a piece of me to the grave with her. I look in the mirror, though, and don't see a single part of her looking back. I'm only left with the ghost of memories that will one day be sucked away by the succubus of time.

I sit in front of my father now at our breakfast table and wonder if he resents me for taking up so much of the limited space and time that he had with the love of his life. It's absurd thinking, I know that. But my mind has always been fractured, distorting the world around me and turning my every thought into my own worst enemy. The mirror is the only place I see the truth—from the vacant stare to the frown lines etching my loneliness and despair permanently into my skin. I plaster on the fakest of smiles now as I pass the pot of coffee to my father. He takes it with a grin and tops off his cup, his golden-brown eyes sparkling with contentment.

"So, are you ready for tonight? I can't believe my little girl is graduating. Seems like just yesterday that your mom and I were crying as we watched you walk into your first day of kindergarten," My father says, reminiscence and sorrow warring in his eyes. My heart clenches every time he speaks of Mom. Each day without her seems to chip away at the life that's left in him.

"I guess so." I try to smile again, but I know it doesn't reach my eyes. My father must notice too, because he gets up from the table and walks over to place a kiss on the top of my head.

"I just wish your mom could have been here to see it," he says softly, tears shining in his eyes. I'm saved from the onslaught of emotions, though, as the doorbell rings. I roll my eyes as I hear the knob turn and the door swing open. What's the point in ringing the doorbell if you're just going to let yourself in anyways?

"Good morning, Miller crew!" A voice as smooth and deep as a serene lake asks. Stormy grey-blue eyes meet my own, and a charming smirk stretches across a perfectly sculpted face. Ryan, our obnoxious neighbor and resident golden boy, winks at me, and I scoff in disgust. His grin widens, and the small dimple on his left cheek pops out, accentuating the sharpness of his cheekbones. I may be able to appreciate how absurdly handsome he is, but his very existence grates my nerves. Ryan runs a hand through the top of his coffee-colored hair, giving it a perfectly messy look. I roll my eyes again as my father stands and greets him with a hug.

"Hey, Ryan. You excited for tonight? It's a big day for both of you!" My dad claps Ryan on the shoulder, giving him a congratulatory squeeze.

"Yes, sir. One step closer to being out on my own," Ryan grins, and my dad chuckles.

"Come on, now. We only get our kiddos with us for a short amount of time before we have to let you loose into the real world. Try not to rush it for us," Dad says and looks at me with a sad smile. I watch the light that Ryan's appearance brought to his face quickly dissipate as a troubled expression takes its place. I've always been envious of the way Ryan makes Dad smile. Mom, too, when she was still alive. He's been here for as long as I can remember, always coming over and crowding our family space. He's been at dinners, holidays, birthdays, and game nights for over a decade. It always felt impossible to shine in Ryan's shadow, though Mom and Dad never seemed to notice. He always seemed to be like a second child to them, and perhaps the preferred one. They were never able to have more children after

I was born and, while Mom never talked about it much, I know it haunted her.

"I wish I could have given you that boy you always dreamed of," I overheard her whisper to Dad once after he spent the evening throwing a football with Ryan. Ryan had come over that day with a black eye and a busted lip after roughhousing too hard with some boys at school. My father had flocked to his side, giving him ice and Tylenol, tending to him like a wounded baby bird. My mother watched them with sorrowful eyes as they threw the football back and forth and then spoke those words to my father that still echo in my mind to this day. From that moment on, I hated Ryan Hartley with every fiber of my being.

"Yeah, yeah," Ryan states with a casual roll of his eyes, pulling me out of my thoughts. I snap back to the conversation at hand when Ryan nods to me.

"I came to see if Samantha wanted to ride to the ceremony with me tonight. You know, save gas and all that." He smirks as if he knows precisely what I'm about to say. He's always gotten off on poking the bear, pestering me until I snap at him. Recently, it hasn't taken much to get me to the point of outburst, and this morning is no different.

"Since when do you give two shits about the environment? And it's Sam to you, Ryan. I'd rather hitchhike and risk catching the eye of a serial killer than ride with you, but thanks." I stand from the table and feel a dark gaze track each step I take.

"Samantha!" My father chides. Disappointment settles in his gaze, a look I'm used to seeing directed at me when Ryan's around. "Don't be rude when he's just being polite. I don't know why you always have to be so sour," he murmurs the last part under his breath before turning back to Ryan. "Thank you for offering Ryan, but you know Sam prefers her solitude," he says with a sad smile. Ryan just tilts his head and smiles at me, a glimmer of victory in his eyes. I flick him off, and his shit-eating grin grows even wider.

"Can't blame a guy for trying," Ryan says casually.

"Will your mom be there tonight?" Dad asks, and I don't miss the way Ryan's smile fades the slightest bit before he plasters it back on.

"Maybe. You know she works a lot." There's a shakiness to his voice that makes an uncomfortable feeling settle in my stomach. Ryan's parents are an enigma; in all the years that they've lived next door, I've seen his mother just a handful of times and his father even less. They've certainly never thrown the football outside with him or even thrown him a birthday party for that matter. Come to think of it, all of Ryan's birthdays were spent at our dinner table with a small homemade cake Mom would decorate with chocolate sprinkles and candles. They would give him a gift each year, and no matter how big or small it was, Ryan would beam at the present like it was Christmas morning.

"Ah, come on. Your child only graduates from high school once. They can let her off work for that," Dad says, skepticism and a hint of judgment lacing his words. I don't think he and Mom have ever cared much for Ryan's parents, and I heard them whispering to each other multiple times over the years about 'what goes on in that house.' As much as I don't like Ryan, I think I like his parents even less. How can someone so reclusive and emotionally stunted create someone as outgoing and thoughtful as Ryan? It repulses me to admit, but Ryan has always brought a light to my parents' eyes when he'd surprise them with their favorite donuts from the bakery in town or bring Mom a new plant for her garden. He'd explain to her precisely why he bought it and just where he thought it would look best in her garden. She would beam at him, and my heart would sink with that familiar feeling of alienation.

Despite my prickly nature toward Ryan, he's shown up on my doorstep on the morning of my birthday for the last three years with my favorite iced hazelnut latte and a carrot cake cupcake. How can someone that thoughtful be the product of two people who never even throw their kid a birthday party?

"I'm sure she'll try to make it," Ryan says, obviously wanting to drop the subject. Dad just nods and tilts his head to the side, giving Ryan an odd look.

"What about your dad? Is he going to be there?" Dad asks, his tone terse in the way it only gets when he speaks of Ryan's father.

"No," Ryan states, refusing to elaborate further. Dad just huffs and shakes his head before clapping Ryan on the shoulder again.

"Well, I'll be there, son. I'll be extra loud for the both of you," he says, turning to look between me and Ryan.

"Great," I murmur, turning to wash the dishes and tuning the rest of their conversation out. Something about my father calling Ryan 'son' sends me spiraling back into that familiar bitter rage.

Sometime later as I'm finishing the dishes, I hear the front door close, and my father reenters the kitchen. I brace myself for the incoming chastisement.

"You should really be nicer to him, Sam. He's only ever been kind to you. I'll never understand why you treat him like he's the enemy," Dad says, disappointment lacing every word. "You never know what someone is going through, Sam. You shouldn't go out of your way to make people's lives more difficult. That's not who we are."

I grind my teeth, refusing to give in to the rage simmering beneath my veins.

"Your mom would have been so happy to watch him walk across that stage with you tonight." And just like that, the rage boils over in an uncontrollable flood. I drop the last dish back into the sink and spin on my father.

"Oh, I'm sure she would have been elated. She would have talked nonstop about how he secured the valedictorian slot and got a scholarship to UGA. It's probably for the best that she wasn't here to see me be waitlisted for the same college." My father's posture stiffens, anger settling in his expression.

"Is that what keeps you up at night, Dad? The fact that Mom is missing all of Ryan's precious milestones. Would her death have been easier for you to handle if she had left behind a son for you to experience all your favorite things with rather than a waste of space daughter who looks and acts nothing like either of you?" The harsh words fall out of me in a river of rage. My father pales, the anger on his face being replaced with utter devastation. Self-hatred slithers through my body and wraps itself around my heart, constricting it tightly.

That familiar dark fog fills my mind, telling me that I'll never be the child they wanted, that I'll never be enough. The urge to release the emotional pain by turning it into a physical one overwhelms me, and the scars on my inner thighs throb. Sometimes, pain is the only thing that can anchor me to this life. Otherwise, I'll fall into the abyss of my dark thoughts and drown in them.

"Oh, Samantha." Dad starts toward me with tears in his beautiful eyes, and it shatters me. I shake my head, the need to release my own pain making my skin vibrate. I can't do this right now. I need to get out of this room before I say something that will shatter my meticulously crafted façade of bitterness and show my father the true poisoning sadness that festers inside of me. I feel one wrong move away from slipping off the edge that I've so carefully walked for years. I sometimes wonder what it would be like to just freefall into that darkness and never see the light again.

"Sam," my dad says softer this time as tears fill my eyes. He reaches out, and I throw my hands up, backing away. I feel like I'm one touch away from shattering into a thousand pieces.

Without another word, I turn and run up the stairs to my room. My father calls after me, but I slam the door and lock it. He won't push the matter right now; he never does. I can hear him ascending the stairs and going down the hall to his own room before gently shutting his door.

The need for release overwhelms me as I walk to my dresser and open the top drawer. I slide my hand under the clothes and pull out the little yellow lighter. My skin vibrates with anticipation as the dark fog encompasses more of my mind. I slide down onto the floor next to my bed and pull my pajama pants down. The scars at the tops of my inner thighs greet me, and my hand shakes as I flick the lighter to life. The small flame dances and welcomes me back as I guide it down to the delicate skin. My vision blurs, and I close my eyes as the heat kisses my thigh. The buzzing in my veins hits a crescendo as a symphony of pain erupts along my skin. The dark fog in my mind begins to recede, and numbness settles over me. I drop the lighter and take a deep breath, the sting in my thigh becoming a familiar comfort.

I observe the angry oblong mark that paints my skin a deep red as my fingers ghost over the old white scars that surround it. I slide my pants back up and pull my knees to my chest. A painful sob racks my body, and the inevitable feeling of shame settles in.

Chapter Two

Ryan

Samantha Grace Miller is the bane of my existence. Living next to her my whole life has felt like my greatest blessing and my biggest curse. Every morning, I wake up and look out my window at hers, wondering how she slept or what she'll decide to wear that day. I've watched her grow over the years from a pigtailed little girl to a beautiful young woman with mesmerizing blonde waves, perfectly pout lips, and delicious curves.

Somewhere along the way, I stopped seeing her as just the girl next door that I liked to pester and started seeing her as an enigma that I wanted to unravel and fall into. Her icy stare as cold as the first winter's snow and petite figure became the center of my teenage fantasies; fantasies that have only intensified over the years.

Watching her has become my favorite pastime, one that has kept me sane when my life in this house became unbearable. I know almost everything there is to know about Sam. I know that she claims that her favorite color is blue, but she secretly loves pink. She likes spicy food and sour candies, and her favorite ice cream is espresso chocolate chunk. She's addicted to coffee and can't live without her hazelnut creamer. She consumes comedy shows like they're her lifeline and has a new book in her hand every other day.

Sam sketches like a Leonardo Da Vinci prodigy, yet she hides most of her work away from the world. I've seen a few of her masterpieces littered around her house when I'd come over for family dinners with Mark and Rose. I'd pick one up and marvel at it before Sam would rip it from my hands and throw it in her sketch folder.

Many times, I've found myself dreaming of the girl in her sketches, the one with the haunted eyes and cracked face staring helplessly at the large wave preparing to crash into her. Her features were so like Sam's that the haunted look on her face furthered my suspicions that Sam's sour personality is more like a protective shield against a wave that she believes will drown her at any moment.

She always seems so lonely, despite the few friends that she's had over the years. Even when she dated that dickhead, Derek, last year, she acted as though it were an obligatory relationship, going through the motions with little to no enjoyment. When I looked out my window one night last summer, I was greeted with the sight of Derek pressing her against the tree right outside her window. His lips were on her neck, her leg hiked around his waist.

Yet, the look on her face lacked fervor as she stared up at the branches, letting him use her body for his fulfillment. Jealousy consumed me as I watched them, unable to take my eyes off the dejected look on her face. Then, her head turned, and her eyes met mine. Heat filled her gaze for the first time, and I could hear her moan under the moonlight. My dick grew hard at the sound, and I had to snatch the curtains shut before I stormed down there and ripped the prick off her.

The day that they broke up may or may not have been the best

PIECES OF ME

day of my life despite knowing that it would make absolutely no difference in how Sam sees me. Like I said, living next to her is a blessing and a curse.

Walking into my house, I'm greeted by an atmosphere in complete juxtaposition to the one next door. While Sam's house is filled with sunlight, plants, and personalized decorations, our home is untidy, the curtains always drawn and not a single family photo in sight.

My mother comes down the stairs in her scrubs as she finishes tying her box-dyed raven hair into a bun. She's grown thinner since my dad left, and the wrinkles around her eyes have deepened significantly.

She meets my gaze as she enters the kitchen and fills her travel mug with coffee. She glances down at my shoes, still wet from my trek across the yard.

"I assume you were next door?" She asks, her voice dripping with distaste. I just nod and sip my own coffee. She scoffs and rolls her eyes.

"I'll never understand your obsession with that family," she states with a shake of her head. I straighten and take a step toward her.

"That family," I begin, setting my mug down and crossing my arms over my chest. "Has been more of a family to me over the past ten years than anyone in this house has," I say pointedly. Hurt flashes across her face, but it's quickly replaced with her usual look of annoyance.

"I'm doing the best I can, Ryan. What more do you want from me?" She asks with an exasperated sigh.

"I don't know, Mom. Perhaps dinner together occasionally instead of you just drinking yourself to sleep on the couch every night? Or maybe you could come to your only son's graduation tonight?" I state, already knowing what her response will be. I can't help that flicker of hope, though, that has me holding my breath.

"You know I have to work, Ryan. Someone has to pay the bills around here. You know, since you ran your father off," my mother says, anger rooted in her words. She snatches her purse off the counter and heads for the door. "There's a twenty on the counter for your dinner. Have a nice graduation," she says, barely sparing me a glance before heading out the door.

My heart sinks as her words echo in my mind. Over the past two years, her bitterness toward me has grown and what little warmth she used to show me has disappeared completely. I thought perhaps her behavior was an effect of the alcohol but to know that she truly blames me for Dad leaving is a level of hurt that I wasn't prepared to face today.

I try to shake the thoughts of my father out of my head as I head upstairs and into my room. When I walk in, I instinctively look across the way to Sam's window where her blinds are up, and the white curtains are parted. Once again, the mere knowledge of her existence next door anchors me and calms the erratic beating of my heart. No matter how much Sam hates me, she and Mark are my family, and I refuse to let anyone or anything take them from me.

Chapter Three

Sam

"Damien Allen Marshall," The principal announces, and sweat gathers on my palms as the boy in front of me walks across the stage to receive his diploma. For the thirtieth time in an hour, I glance around the theater, looking for any sign of my father. Ryan sits in the front row of the student section, the gold medallion hanging from his neck illuminating the small flecks of gold in his grey-blue eyes. His head turns under my gaze and worry seeps into his usually relaxed features. His eyes silently question me, and I answer with a small shrug that does nothing to push down the boulder sitting in my throat.

"Samantha Grace Miller." With a deep breath, I plaster on my best smile and walk across the stage. I wait for the roar of my father's usual embarrassing celebratory yodel, but it never comes. My hands begin to tremble as I take my seat again.

He didn't come. My father, the only person I have left in this world, isn't here. My words to him this morning echo in my mind, and nausea rolls through me. I hurt my father so awfully, he couldn't even stand to see me graduate. I press a hand to my mouth to suppress the sob trying to escape. I bite my cheek until I taste blood, and I focus on the slight pain as the graduation carries on.

Right when the ceremony ends, Ryan crowds my space. His tall frame looms over me, and I try to swallow past that still unmoving lump in my throat.

"Where's your dad?" He asks. His eyes scan my face in a way that makes me feel stripped bare. My spine straightens, and I school my features. If anyone ever truly saw beneath the wall of ice that I present, they would be absolutely mortified.

"He didn't come, thanks to you," I declare venomously. Ryan flinches back and blinks at me as if I've suddenly grown another head. My words aren't fair or even honest. Yet once they're out there, I can't help but double down, trying to fault Ryan for my colossal fuck up.

"Me?" His voice cracks slightly, the worry on his face shifting to panic.

"Yes, you. If you hadn't come over this morning and once again inserted yourself into our lives, he and I wouldn't have had that stupid argument, and he would be here." I take a step closer to Ryan and look up at him with a menacing gaze.

"Because of you, I had to walk across that stage to the sound of silence and be reminded once again that I'm in this alone." I look around for anyone coming to celebrate with Ryan but see no one. "Where's your family, huh? Why don't you go find your own parents and leave mine the hell alone?" Hurt flashes in his eyes, and his sharp jaw ticks.

"You don't know what the fuck you're talking about, Sam," he growls, his eyes darkening with anger.

"Oh, I see. Your parents don't give you enough attention, so you feel the need to force yourself into my family. Well, guess what, Ryan? He didn't show up for you, either," I snarl. Ryan's hand curls into a fist at his side, anger radiating off him in waves.

"You know, I've put up with your callous bullshit for years. I've tried to be your friend and find ways to make you smile or laugh, to break through that wall of armor that you cast out to the world. But if you keep up this heartless act, you really will end up bitter and alone with no one around to see the real you," Ryan says, looking at me as if he's peering into my soul.

"Fuck you, Ryan," I grit out before turning and storming out of the auditorium without looking back.

--

Less than twenty minutes later, I throw my car in park and slam the door. My heels clack aggressively against the pavement as I stomp up the driveway, the Georgia heat making my dress stick to my body. As I open the front door, the rage from earlier bubbles inside of me, begging for release and causing the burn on my thigh to throb. Stepping inside, I don't find my father sitting in the living room watching his usual football recordings like I expected.

"Dad?" I call out for him, but deafening silence is the only response. I walk into the dark kitchen, finding no sign of him, and then head upstairs to his room.

"Dad, are you in there?" I ask as I knock on the bedroom door. Again, silence greets me. An icy feeling wars with the rage in my veins as I swallow and knock again. "Dad?" My voice trembles.

"Look, I know I said some truly horrible things earlier, but I didn't mean them. I'm so sorry, please come out so we can talk." I wait for the sound of my father shuffling to the door on the other side, but it never comes. I bang on the door this time as the rage starts to win out the war being fought inside of me.

"The silent treatment, Dad, really? I know I said some shitty things, but if anyone has the right to give someone the silent treatment, it's me. How could you not come to my graduation? You knew Mom wouldn't be there, and you left me there with no one. I never took you for a cold person, Dad, but that's fucking heartless," I snarl. I brace for the rebuke he will surely give me for cursing, but my erratic breaths are the only sound filling the space. "Dad!" I yell, banging on the door.

"Fuck it," I whisper, reaching out to turn the handle. The door creaks as I push it open and step into the room. My parents' bed sits perfectly made, illuminated only by the strands of moonlight seeping through the blinds.

"Dad?" My voice comes out in a shaky breath as I scan the room for any sign of him. I walk closer to the bed and come to a violent halt when my father's face looks up at me from the floor. His body lay next to the bed, and my eyes latch onto the still expanse of his broad chest. Sweat trickles down my palms as I wait for his chest to rise and fall. It never does. His open eyes stare up at me in a glazed expression. The face that once looked warm and vibrant looks as if it has solidified into a wax statue, freezing the look of pain on his face for eternity.

"No, no, no, no, no, no." I stumble forward and crash my knees against the hard floor next to my father. "Dad, wake up!" I exclaim as denial seeps into my bones. With a trembling hand, I reach for his face. My breathing stops as my fingertips brush against icy skin.

"Oh god, no. Dad! DAD!!!" I scream, fisting my hands into his shirt and trying to shake him awake. His head rolls to the side with the movement, and dizzying nausea slams into me. My tears come down onto his shirt in a torrent of despair, and I let my head fall onto his wet shirt. The unnatural stiffness of his chest rips a cry from me so painful that it feels as if my throat is being sliced open. I scream until the bellows turn into hoarse whimpers, and my vision darkens around the edges. Laying there with my father, I slowly close my eyes and let the void finally pull me under.

Chapter Four

Ryan

If there's one person in this world who can take a good day and turn it into a shit show of emotions, it's Samantha fucking Miller. For years, I have tried relentlessly to pull a little bit of sunshine from the depths of her darkness, but the girl is a damn blackout curtain refusing to allow even a sliver of light in. Still, I can't help the way heat rushes through my body when her icy gaze meets mine or when she bites back at me with her witty retorts. Tonight, however, I wanted to ring her damn neck. How dare she blame me for her fucking behavior? I would never jeopardize her relationship with her father. Hell, he was all I was going to have there, too. Instead, I walked across that stage with my chin up and accepted my diploma with just the hoots and hollers of my teammates and friends. No family in sight.
I look at the time on my phone as I toss in bed for the thousandth time. It's just after midnight, and Sam's damn words are haunting me. With a resigned huff, I throw the covers off and stand. I put on a shirt and shoes and stomp down the stairs. I don't care if she's sleeping or not—Samantha is about to hear every fucking thing I think about her sour existence. I pass the

living room on my way out and spot my mother passed out on the sofa. Empty beer bottles litter the floor next to her, and she's still dressed in her hospital scrubs. I stop beside the couch and lean over to flick off the lamp. Grabbing a nearby blanket, I drape it over her before gathering the bottles off the floor and taking them to the trash.

Disgust and sympathy battle inside of me as I walk past her sleeping form again to exit the front door. Her pain is a palpable being that has settled in our house since Dad left, yet I can't fathom how his absence was somehow more damaging to her than the loss of her relationship with her son.

I shake my head, jog across the lawn and approach the large tree next to Sam's room. On sleepless nights, I would sit next to my window and count the stars in the sky like I'd count the days until I could leave this town. On a few of those nights, I would get the rare sighting of a petite blonde climbing out of her window and carefully down the large tree. She would tiptoe to her car and disappear into the night. I would sit there until she came back each time, ensuring that she was safe.

Now, I take a page out of her book and pull my body up the branches, my muscles contracting and bulging beneath my clothes. I get to the window and peer inside. Sam has always left her curtains open for some infuriating reason. There was no escaping her. Even in my own home, I could look across at her window and see her reading or sketching. Sometimes, I would be cursed with a view of her sitting on the bench at her window sobbing. My fingers would twitch at my side with the need to wipe her tears away and pull her safely into my chest.

Looking into her window now, though, I see nothing. Her bed is perfectly made, and her sketchpads sit in a small stack on her desk. Her car sits in the driveway next to her dad's, so I know she's here. The branch creaks beneath my weight as I shift forward and test the window. It slides up easily. I grit my teeth at her carelessness. Fucking Samantha, always a breath away from disaster. Maybe sneaking into her window in the middle of the night will teach her to keep the damn thing locked. I slide easily into her room and listen for the sounds of life coming from anywhere in the house. Absolute silence greets me. Sam isn't the type to fall asleep on the couch, but I creep out of the room and down the stairs anyways to check. The downstairs is empty and unease creeps into my bones. The front door is unlocked, and I wonder if perhaps she had someone pick her up. My hands curl into fists on their own accord at the idea of some random guy getting to take her somewhere in the middle of the night.

I need to get out of here, though, before Mark comes down and shoots me like I'm some intruder. I suppose I am, but I'm a harmless one. Pulling out my phone, I open Sam's contact and hit the call button. I head for the front door when a ringing sound echoes the one in my ear. I lower my phone and listen. The sound comes again from somewhere upstairs, and I make my way toward it. The ringing stops when I hit the top of the stairs, so I hang up and dial again. The ringtone plays louder this time as I step closer to her parents' bedroom. I knock on the door, cautiously calling out for her. Ringing is the only answer, and the knot in my stomach triples in size.

Turning the knob, I step inside and move across the room until I see Sam's phone lying on the floor at the foot of the bed. My contact flashes across the screen, and I end the call. I pick up her phone and take another step forward, halting when I see a socked foot poking out from the far side of the bed. Time slows and my heart thumps erratically in my chest. There on the floor, lays Mark's still body, his skin a lifeless grey and his eyes vacant. My heart shatters into a million pieces at the sight of Sam curled up against her father, still dressed in her ceremony dress and heels. Her head lies on his chest with her eyes closed, and black streaks of mascara paint her cheeks.

"Sam?" My voice is unrecognizable as I try to wake her. She doesn't move, and fear electrifies me. *"Fuck, please don't be dead,"* I think as I rush forward and fall to my knees beside her. With trembling fingers, I reach out and touch her neck. The warmth that greets my own kickstarts my heart, and I release a shaky breath when the thump of Sam's pulse beats against my fingers.

Unsure of what else to do, I grab my phone and dial 9-1-1.

"9-1-1, what's the location of your emergency?" The operator prompts. I quickly recite the address of the house that has been more of a home to me than my own for the past fifteen years.

"What's your emergency at this location, sir?"

"I—um—," I stutter as I stare down at Mark's lifeless body. This man has been the brightest spot of my day for so many years. He's full of kindness and knowledge, and he gives the best goddamn hugs. He's been more of a father to me than my own has ever been. He can't be dead. How the hell am I supposed to say something that can't possibly be true?

"Sir?" The operator asks again, and I swallow the acidic taste in my mouth.

"I came to check on my neighbors and found one of them unresponsive. The other seems to be in shock," I relay with a voice much steadier than I feel.

"Okay, sir. EMS and police have been dispatched to your location. You said one person was unresponsive. Can you tell if they are breathing?"

My grip tightens on the phone as I look down at Mark's rigid form. I close my eyes and force the truth through gritted teeth. "No. No, he's gone." The words puncture my heart, creating a wound that I know will never heal.

"Do you see any causes of injury or any weapons in the area?" The dispatcher asks calmly.

"No, nothing like that. I—I think he had a heart attack." The words sound robotic, and I barely listen to the dispatcher's last words before I hang up. When I look back at the scene on the floor, I find a pair of baby blue eyes staring up at me as Sam lifts her head and blinks in confusion.

"Ryan?" Sam's voice shakes and lacks the disdain that usually accompanies her use of my name.

"Hey, Sam." I crouch in front of her and hold my hand out. "Do you think we could stand up and go downstairs to wait on the ambulance? I already called, and they should be here any minute," I say, my heart pounding in my chest. Sam's brows crease further, and that acidic taste crawls back up my throat.

"Called them? What for?" She asks with a slight chuckle. The sound unnerves me, and that wound in my heart deepens.

"Your dad, Sam," I whisper with a nod to the body on the floor. She turns to look beside her and starts to vigorously shake her head.

"No, no. He's fine. He's just sleeping. Right, Dad?" Sam says as she leans down to brush the hair back off his forehead. His cloudy eyes stare up at her, and I reach over to close them. The icy skin sends nausea rolling through me.

"What the hell are you doing? I said he's fine!" Sam exclaims and pushes me back away from her. I almost fall on my ass at the sudden movement.

Sam leans back over her father and rubs a thumb gently over his cheekbone.

"Come on, Dad. Wake up," She whispers. My soul shatters into irreparable shards as I stand and pull Sam's small form off her father. A screech pierces my ears, and she begins flailing against me. I grit my teeth as her heels slam into my legs, and her nails scrape against my arms.

"Put me down! He's fine!" She screams while kicking and punching every part of my body she can reach. I wrap my arms tighter around her and pull her back flush against my chest.

"He's gone, Samantha," I growl into her ear. "He's dead. Wake the fuck up and see that." My words feel harsh, but I don't know how else to shake her from this state of shock. Sam whimpers and goes slack in my arms.

"I hate you, Ryan. I hate you so fucking much," She whispers as her head falls back against my shoulder. I hold her tighter and kiss the top of her head.

"I know, Sam. I know."

Chapter Five

Sam

My father is dead.

I sit on the sofa with my knees pulled tightly to my chest as an icy grip wraps its hand around my heart. A thick blanket falls across my knees, and I look up to see Ryan standing in front of me. I thought he would have left by now, but he stands with his arms crossed and watches as the gurney carrying my dad exits the house. He walks to the front door and speaks with an officer before closing it and turning the lock.

"They said the coroner will release his body to the funeral home of your choosing tomorrow," Ryan says as he sits on the couch next to me. He doesn't look at me, just sits forward with his elbows on his knees and clasps his hands together tightly. Fresh scratches mark his arms from my feeble attempts to escape his strong hold earlier. I just wanted to be with my dad, to lay with him until my skin and bones were as cold as his. I don't want to be here in this house without his laugh, his stories, or the smell of his amazing cooking. I thought I was lonely before, but that word doesn't do justice to how I feel now. I feel as if I am nothing, just a carcass of grief and darkness.

"What were you doing here?" I ask hoarsely. My throat is raw from screaming and crying, but the pain when I speak is almost comforting. Physical pain has always been a way for me to clear the fog of despair, even if just for a moment. It anchors me when I feel myself drifting too far.

"I was pissed at you," Ryan says and turns to look at me. He looks broken in a way I've never seen him. Unshed tears glimmer in his eyes, and his usually perfect hair looks as if he's been pulling at it.

"I came over to confront you about what you said earlier tonight, but I suppose it doesn't matter now," He explains with a sad smile.

"So, you just let yourself into our house at midnight just to yell at me?" My lips curve in the smallest of smiles at that ridiculousness.

"Well, who can turn down a little moonlight trespassing when your unlocked bedroom window makes it so easy?" Ryan turns to look at me with a mischievous grin. My mouth falls open in surprise, and my eyes widen as they take in his tall frame and muscular build.

"You—you climbed into my window in the middle of the night to yell at me?! Are you psychotic?!" I squeak in disbelief.

"And I'd do it again knowing what I know now. Knowing that you needed me." His eyes bore into mine like he's searching for something I'm not aware of.

"I didn't--," I begin but stop myself. I can't possibly tell him that I didn't need him, that I was perfectly content to waste away lying there with my dad until the reaper came for me, too.

"I'm sorry." I say instead. "For what I said after the ceremony. It wasn't fair, and it wasn't true. I'm the reason he didn't come to graduation. I'm the reason he was here all alone with no one to help him. That's on me, not you. I'm so sorry, Ryan." The truth tastes bitter in my mouth, and self-loathing slithers through my veins. It's a familiar feeling but strikes with a new intensity now.

"It's no one's fault, Sam. Fights happen, parents and kids bicker. There isn't a single person out there who hasn't said something they regret in the heat of the moment. You had no way of knowing this would happen." Ryan looks at me with that piercing gaze again that makes me feel stripped bare and says, "All you can do now is spend every day from here on out keeping his memory alive and making him proud. Just like you've been doing for your mom."

I stay silent at his words because there's no world in which I feel like I've made her proud, especially now. She would be so ashamed of the way I spoke to my father earlier and absolutely devastated to know that he died heartbroken and alone.

"I think I'm cursed," I murmur, and Ryan eyes me worriedly. Sometimes, I feel like a disease, infecting everyone around me with sadness and destruction.

"You aren't cursed, Sam. Death is the only guarantee in this life; it comes for each of us eventually. You didn't cause Rose or Mark's deaths, and you couldn't have prevented them. Don't blame yourself for this, Sam." Ryan gives me a hard look, leaving no room for debate. I just nod and sniffle, though his words don't change the feelings inside of me.

"Look, I can go with you tomorrow if you want. You know, to make the arrangements and everything. I know you guys didn't have much family around here, and I don't think you should do this alone, Sam," Ryan offers. My heart clenches at the reminder of what tomorrow will bring, and the idea of facing it alone tiptoes me closer to the edge of insanity.

"Um, yeah. I'd appreciate that. Thank you, Ryan," I say as I lean forward and place my hand on his clasped ones. I feel his tendons twitch beneath my touch, and a smile creeps onto his face. Just this morning, his presence filled me with rage and bitterness, but now, there's a comfort to having him next to me.

"Wow, I didn't know you could say my name without it dripping in hatred," He teases. I roll my eyes and remove my hand. I shake my head and look around at the large space I grew up in. There's an iciness to the air now, a lack of warmth and love left behind in the absence of my parents.

Ryan stands and surveys me with that scrutinous gaze of his as though he's reading my thoughts. "Are you going to be alright here by yourself? I can stay here on the couch if it would help you feel more comfortable," he offers kindly.

I take in Ryan's 6'2 frame and then look down at our small couch. I almost laugh at the image my mind creates of him trying to lay across it, long legs dangling over the edge and neck bent at an uncomfortable angle.

"No," I shake my head. "I'll be okay." The lie tumbles out of my mouth with ease.

"Thank you for everything tonight, and I'm really sorry for how I acted today. I know I haven't always been the nicest person, but I appreciate you being willing to help me," I say as I push the blanket off and stand. I turn to head towards the front door to see him out, but a warm hand on my wrist stops me. I turn back to see Ryan looking down at me.

"I'll always be here for you, Sam," he says in a voice that roots me in place, and his thumb softly moves across my wrist to settle on my pulse. Ryan holds it there for a moment before releasing my arm and moving to the door. The absence of his touch sends an odd feeling through me, and there's no way in hell I'm trying to evaluate that tonight.

"I'll see you at noon, okay? Then we can head over to the funeral home. Try and get some rest. Lock up behind me, and don't forget the window," he says with a wink before opening and shutting the door.

I small smile creeps onto my face as I walk over and slide the lock into place. It quickly dissipates though as the bolting sound echoes in my ears. The chill of the house settles deep in my bones, and the loneliness that lives in me becomes a crushing weight that steals my breath.

I've only ever had a few friends, and even with them, I felt like an outsider. I was never the one invited first or the friend everyone wanted at sleepovers. I've aways been the afterthought friend, and I imagine it has something to do with my joyously sunny disposition. When my mom died, though, I withdrew completely from the few people I had left. Dad was the only one left standing to deal with my temperamental existence. Until now.

I try to take a steadying breath as the emptiness of my life becomes painfully clear. A horrible sob escapes me, and I fall to my knees. The impact reverberates through my bones, and I scream over and over for the second time tonight.

Sometime later, I pull myself off the floor and upstairs to the bathroom. I fill the tub with steaming hot water and slowly take my dress and heels off. Looking in the mirror, I gasp at the sight that greets me. My hair is a mess of frizzy disheveled waves, and mascara streaks track from my puffy eyes down to my jawline. I look certifiably insane. It's a wonder Ryan was able to look at me and have a serious conversation without laughing in my face.

I turn away from my reflection and step into the scorching water. The sting on my skin grounds me in this moment, and I sink into it. I lift my leg up out of the water and use my foot to turn off the tap. The surface of the water brushes against my thigh where the small scars decorate the skin. I slide it back beneath the water and sink all the way down to my ears.

I lay there just staring at the ceiling while the water creates a cocoon of silence around me. The warmth surrounding me feels peaceful and welcoming like the void that often calls to me. I wonder how easy it would be to fall into it and just make it all stop.

I close my eyes and slide completely under the surface. Water invades my nostrils, but I hold my breath and anchor myself in place with my hands on either side of the tub. My lungs begin to burn as the seconds tick by. A dizzying darkness creeps into my brain, and my head starts to pound.

"Please just take me," I beg the universe as me lungs scream at me to get up and breathe. I refuse and push harder on the sides of the tub until I feel my palms bruising. My eyes begin to open and roll, the water stinging them.

"Please take me with you," I plea as the image of my father comes into my mind. My mother joins the image and wraps an arm around him. They look so happy and in love. The way they were with each other was a beautiful thing to witness.

"All you can do now is keep their memory alive," my brain reminds me of Ryan's words. The darkness starts to overcome my parents' image in my mind, and I open my mouth to stop it. Water rushes into my nostrils and mouth, and I lurch up choking. My coughs turn into dry heaves, as the numbness in my limbs starts to dissipate. I sit there for a moment just watching the water rock against the edge of the tub. Exhaustion barrels into me as I stand and exit the bath. I forgo a towel and let my wobbly legs carry me to my bed across the hall. I leave a trail of wet footprints as I climb into the bed and pull the covers over my naked body. Closing my eyes, I succumb to the fatigue and let it pull me into unconsciousness.

Chapter Six

Sam

My head pulses as my body returns to consciousness after hours of dreamless sleep. I groan, refusing to open my eyes just yet.

"What did I say about leaving your window unlocked, Samantha?" A deep voice demands. My eyes fly open, and a scream leaves my throat. I sit up abruptly, slamming my bare back against the headboard and pulling the covers tightly over my chest. My erratic heartbeat tries to return to normal as I take in Ryan standing at the foot of my bed, but the sight just makes my heart pulse to a wilder rhythm. He's dressed in dark jeans and a maroon henley that accentuates his chiseled chest, shoulders, and biceps. His crossed arms put the muscles on full display as he cocks his head and raises an eyebrow at me.

"What the hell is wrong with you?!" I yell, grabbing the pillow next to me and chucking it at his arrogant face. He swats it away and chuckles, the sound luscious and hypnotic.

"You can't just go around breaking into people's homes, Ryan." I grip the covers tighter, making sure every part of my naked body is covered from his sultry gaze. I've always been able to appreciate that Ryan was good looking despite my dislike of him personally. The last day, however, has put a magnifying glass to his every feature in a way that leaves me breathless.

"Not people's homes, Samantha, just yours." He moves to rest his hands on the edge of my bed and leans forward. "And how can I resist when you leave it unlocked just for me?" He winks, and my cheeks flush with heat. God, I can't stand him.

"It wasn't for you, and don't call me Samantha. Now, please leave so I can get dressed," I try to say sternly, but it comes out shaky. Ryan must notice because his lips quirk before he turns and leaves the room, shutting the door behind him.

Twenty minutes later, I come downstairs and instantly moan at the decadent smell of fresh coffee. The scent fills my nostrils and wraps around me like a warm embrace. Ryan's eyes widen at the sound, and I blush for the second time this morning. God, I just need to get this day over with and get him out of my space.

I grab a mug and fill it with coffee and a splash of hazelnut creamer before taking a long sip. The comforting taste rushes through my veins, and I close my eyes and moan again.

"Do you and your coffee need some alone time?" Ryan quips.

"Preferably, yes, if that means you'll go home," I say, unable to resist. The ease of our usual banter is an odd comfort. Ryan puts a hand over his heart and gasps dramatically.

"Ouch, that hurts. But no can do, Samantha. You've got one hell of a day ahead of you, and I, in good conscience, can't let you do it alone," Ryan says. I'm about to chide him for the use of my full name again but stop myself when his relaxed expression turns serious.

"Any idea what your dad wanted for his service?" He asks. I nod and swallow the quickly forming lump in my throat.

"Yeah. We, uh, talked about it after mom died. He wanted it short and sweet, and he wanted to be laid to rest right next to her,"

I say. I remember insisting that we didn't need to talk about it because there was no way in hell he would be dying anytime soon. That was just five months ago.

Once again, the entity of time laughed in my fucking face.

"He also said that if something happened to him, I need to call his friend Dave regarding his will and assets. He owns a law firm in town. Maybe we can stop by there after the funeral home," I suggest. I don't want to be doing any of this, but I'll do whatever I can to honor my dad's wishes. It's what he deserves.

"Of course, yeah," Ryan says without question. "We can go wherever you need." He smiles softly as he sets his mug in the sink and grabs his keys off the counter.

I fill another cup of coffee into a travel mug and pour in the creamer. Today is, without a doubt, a double caffeine day.

We head to the front door, and I stop in the foyer to grab my purse and check my appearance in the large mirror. My blonde waves are pulled up in a high ponytail, and my face is bare. Puffy blue eyes stare back at me as I make sure my clothing is funeral home appropriate. My black top fits snugly to my chest, and my light blue maxi skirt sits high on my waist and falls past my knees. White flowers decorate the skirt, and black wedges complete the look.

"Ready?" Ryan asks as he holds the front door open.

"Yeah, I'm ready," I answer, though I don't feel the slightest bit ready. We exit the house, and I lock the door behind us. The Georgia heat greets us immediately as we walk down the steps to the driveway. Ryan's black truck sits behind my small Kia. I pause as he goes to open the passenger door of the truck.

"We can take my car," I say, trying not to be more of an imposition than I already am. Ryan just stares at me while holding the door open.

"I'm here to help you today, so let me help, Sam," He states sternly. I let out a resigned huff as I walk forward and climb into the passenger seat. Ryan smiles in that arrogant way of his and shuts the door behind me. He walks around the front and climbs into the driver's side. He starts the car with the push of a button, and the engine purrs to life. I watch his forearms flex as he puts the truck in reverse and guides us out of the driveway. I turn away before he catches me staring and focus my attention on the passing trees.

My mother always loved the pine trees that lined the entrance of our neighborhood and ogled at the plant nursery down the road from our house. She had a way with nature that gave her an ethereal glow anytime she encountered it. I hope she's surrounded by evergreens and flowers wherever she is now and welcomes my father into her field of eternal peace with open arms.

Fifteen minutes later, Ryan navigates the truck into the lot of the funeral home. Sweat begins to gather in my palms as a sense of déjà vu strikes. Not that long ago, I had been here with Dad making Mom's arrangements. I had told myself that day that if I could just get through her service, I wouldn't have to see this place again for a long time. I couldn't have been more wrong.

Ryan exits the truck, comes around to my side, and opens the door for me. I wipe my palms on my skirt before stepping out. The May heat wraps around us with suffocating intensity as we head into the old building. My steps falter and come to a halt as we get closer to the main room. Ryan's hand comes to rest on my back, and I tilt my head up to look at him. His grey-blue eyes anchor me in place as his thumb gently strokes the bottom of my back.

"Hey, you've got this," Ryan states with a confidence that I don't feel. "You're not alone," he says softly. I just nod, not trusting myself to speak as his words send a new wave of emotions through me. Then, I turn to lead us into the place that meant nothing to me six months ago but will now haunt me for the rest of my life.

Chapter Seven

Sam

Two hours later, Ryan and I climb back into his truck and head to Dave's office. We say nothing as we both swallow our emotions and stuff them deep inside ourselves. I tried not to look at Ryan too much during the funeral planning because the glistening of tears in his eyes and the slight tremble in his chin was making it impossible to keep my own shit together.

The silence drags on as we pull up to the small brick building next to the town square. Hahira, Georgia doesn't offer much but the quaint little downtown area has a unique charm. Ryan slides the truck into park, and I exit the vehicle before he can try and open my door for me again. His chivalrous actions today are throwing off our usually discourteous dynamic, and I desperately need to hang on to a sliver of normalcy. Ryan doesn't seem to notice, though, as he heads to the building and holds open the front door. I roll my eyes and walk past, ignoring the butterflies that his smug smile sends fluttering in my stomach.

I approach the reception desk and am greeted by a beautiful older woman with dark skin and white hair. Her brown eyes are filled with a warm kindness as she looks up at me.

"Hello, how can I help you today?" She asks, and her voice is just as comforting as her wide smile. Her presence puts me at ease. The gold nametag clipped to her blouse reads "Donna," and her desk is crowded with frames of family photos.

"My name is Samantha Miller," I begin nervously. "I'm here to see Mr. Dave Williford. My father passed away yesterday, and he told me on numerous occasions to make sure I came here immediately if anything ever happened to him." My voice begins to break with those words, and I clear my throat. I can feel Ryan's presence at my back, and I find an odd comfort in it.

The kind woman gives us a sad smile and says, "I'm so sorry for your loss. I'll let Mr. Williford know you're here. He'll be with you in just a moment." She stands from her chair and walks down the small hallway before knocking on a door and disappearing into what I assume is Mr. Williford's office.

Ryan and I stand in the reception area and wait, his hand coming to rest on my back and grounding me in his touch.

A few minutes later, a short older man with salt and pepper hair and a handsomely wrinkled face comes out of the office with Donna by his side. She takes her seat back at the desk as he approaches us.

"Hello, Samantha. I'm Mr. Williford, but you can call me Dave. I'm so sorry to hear about your father's passing. He was one of the most genuine people I've ever had the pleasure of knowing," Dave says, and I can feel the sadness in his words. My father was a larger-than-life man—someone who left an impact on every person he met.

"Thank you," I tell him. "I'm not sure why I'm here though. I assume my dad wanted me to speak with you about his will?"

"Yes, yes. Your father set up his last will and testament with us and entrusted me with making sure you received a few important documents. If you'll follow me, we can get everything taken care of." He turns and heads back into his office. I follow with Ryan on my heels.

We enter the small room, and both take a seat in the leather chairs sitting in front of Dave's desk. He pulls a file cabinet open and rifles through it for a moment before walking back to his chair with a folder in hand.

"Now, your father paid off the mortgage on the family home when your mother passed and put the remainder of her life insurance policy into an account in your name. His policy will be added to that account per his wishes when those funds are released," Dave explains as he sits. My stomach sinks at the levity of his words, reminding me of just how alone I am now.

"He had already set aside the funds needed for his services after your mother's passing, so you don't need to worry about that. I will start the paperwork to transfer ownership of the home into your name. I will just need a few documents from you and your ID." He slides a paper to me across the desk. "This is the banking information for your account. You can go there and get the access number to log into the mobile app and receive your card. Other than that, your father wanted me to ensure you received this." Dave pulls a tiny manilla envelope out of the file and passes it to me. It fits in the palm of my hand as I open it. A small silver key falls into my lap, and I pick it up to inspect it. There's no logo, just a small circular keychain connected to it with the number 33 written on it.

"What is this?" I ask, looking at Dave. I turn to Ryan as well who leans forward and plucks the envelope out of my lap, flipping it over to check for any other contents. Nothing comes out, and Ryan just shrugs at me.

"Your father has a safety deposit box at the bank just a couple blocks down from here. I don't know what the box contains, only that key opens it." He nods to the key in my hand. "I was instructed to make sure you got that key and knew where to go with it. He was very adamant about that wish." Dave stands and places the rest of the file back in his cabinet.

"I'll get all the legalities sorted for you over the next few days. You don't need to worry about any of that. Just try to take care of yourself, Sam. And you sir," Dave nods to Ryan who stands from his chair. "Look out for her, okay?"

Ryan nods stiffly and says, "I will, sir." They shake hands, and Dave turns to look at me again. I stay frozen in my seat, staring at the key in my hand.

"Take a few minutes in here if you need. I have an appointment starting in a moment, but I have another room I can use," he says kindly, but I shake my head. I don't want to impose any more than I already have, and the key feels like it's burning a hole in my hand. My curiosity pushes me to my feet.

"No, sir. We've taken up enough of your time already. I really appreciate your help and for making sure my father's wishes were honored. You have no idea how much it means to me," I say genuinely. Dave nods with a small smile before ushering us to the door.

Ryan and I walk out of the office and into the parking lot. We climb into the truck, and Ryan starts the engine as I inspect the key once more.

"Mind if we make one more stop?" I ask, nodding in the direction of the federal bank just up the road. Ryan's eyes sparkle with excitement.

"Oh, hell yeah. I need to see what type of treasures Mark had that he felt needed to be kept under lock and key in a guarded bank," he says energetically. I laugh nervously at his words, an uneasy feeling settling in my gut. Just a couple minutes later, we pull up to the bank and park.

"I doubt it's some treasure or anything exciting. If anything, I bet it will be those old collection coins with all the unique years on them," I state, but even I'm not convinced by my own words. Ryan shakes his head as we get out of the car and head into the building.

"No, it's definitely going to be a rare family jewel or a one-of-a-kind football card that worth hundreds of thousands." Ryan eyes twinkle with intrigue, his excitement palpable.

I laugh at the idea of my dad having something worth hundreds of thousands just lying around. No, he certainly would have told me about something like that.

"I highly doubt that," I say, and Ryan huffs.

"A man can dream," he grumbles as we approach the check in desk.

I check us in and wait for a clerk to come and take us to the safety deposit box room. Ryan steps closer to me as people filter in and out of the bank.

"Hey," he says, pulling my attention up to his handsome face. "Maybe after this, we can go grab a burger together at The Buzz." He looks nervous as he says it, as if he's asking about more than just food. I consider him for a moment and open my mouth to answer when a clerk approaches us.

"Let's talk about it after, okay?" I say as we follow the clerk into a large room with lockboxes. Ryan nods with a small smile and follows me to where the clerk stands in front of lockbox #33. I thank him, and he leaves us in privacy to open it. I push the key in and unlock the small door then reach in and pull the black box out. My hands shake as I set the box on the table in the center of the room and put the key into the lock. Holding my breath, I turn the key. Ryan comes to stand behind me, his warm breath against my neck as I lift the lid on the box. Confusion and unease settle in my bones.

"What is all this?" Ryan asks, reaching over me to pull a single piece of paper out of the box. He holds it up and looks at me. "Why is your birth certificate in a lock box with--," He trails off as he picks up the last two items in the box. "A photo of a woman that looks eerily similar to you holding a baby and a faded sticky note with a number on it?" Ryan's eyes flick between me and the polaroid as I try to process the contents of the box.

"I don't—I don't know," I admit. I check the box again, but there's nothing else in it. I turn to Ryan and grab the paper from his hand. My birth certificate looks normal with my name and my parents' names exactly where they should be.

"The top of this page labels it as an amended birth certificate, but that just means it's a copy, right?" I ask, and Ryan shakes his head.

"I don't think so," he says, his eyebrows furrowed in confusion. He holds up the sticky note. "Maybe this number will have the answers. I mean, your dad felt it was important enough to be left in this box for you. Maybe we should head back to your house and call it."

I snatch the note from his hand and pull my phone out of my pocket.

"No, I'm calling them now." I grab the polaroid and birth certificate off the table and walk out of the bank with Ryan hot on my heels. As soon as we make it outside, the phone is pressed to my ear. It rings twice before a woman answers.

"Hello, this is Grace." The voice is timid, older, and not one that I recognize.

"Grace?" I ask, confusion lacing my words as I stop suddenly on the sidewalk. Ryan stares at me with the same perplexed look I know is on my face.

"Yes, and who am I speaking to?" Grace questions. There's no rudeness to her words, and something about her voice makes me drop my guard slightly.

"My name is Samantha. I found your number in a lock box. My dad passed away yesterday, and he felt it was very important that I find your number. Do you have any idea why that is?" My voice sounds accusatory, though I don't mean for it to.

There's a long pause for a moment, and I wonder if she's hung up when she suddenly says, "Was there anything else in this box, Samantha?"

Her question throws me, but I nod before remembering she can't see me.

"Yes, there was a photo of a woman holding a baby and an amended birth certificate." Saying those words out loud shifts something inside of me, and a sense of foreboding settles over me. "Do you have any idea why those three things would be in a lock box in a bank for who knows how long?" I ask her shakily. Grace sighs over the line before speaking.

"What were your parents' names, honey?" She questions, though something tells me she already knows.

"Mark and Rose Miller," I answer. That sense of foreboding increases substantially when Grace sighs again.

"I worked with Mark and Rose about eighteen years ago, Samantha. I can only assume they left those contents for you because they wanted you to know the truth."

"And what is the truth?" I ask with a trembling voice. Ryan steps closer to me and rests his hand on my arm.

Grace clears her throat before speaking the words that set fire to the life I thought I knew.

"You're adopted, Samantha, and I helped them to bring you home."

Chapter Eight

Ryan

Something is very wrong. Sam isn't moving, just standing there staring at the ground with the phone still pressed tightly to her ear. I can hear the woman's voice on the other end repeating Sam's name with increasing concern. I couldn't hear what they were talking about before Sam resorted to this statuesque state, but whatever that woman said seems to have fractured her in an irreparable way.

"Sam," I say gruffly while snapping my fingers in front of her face. She doesn't move. The small little breath she takes in is the only sign of life in her body right now.

"Fuck," I growl as I snatch the phone from her ear and place it against my own.

"Samantha!" The woman exclaims again. Her voice is dripping with urgency and fear.

"This is her boyfriend, Ryan." Okay, that might be a lie, but if I'm going to get her to tell me about something that was important enough to be put in a locked box in a federal bank, then the truth just isn't going to cut it.

"Is she okay?" She asks, but I don't answer as I take in Sam's frozen form. She sure as hell is not okay.

"What the hell did you say to her?" I demand. My heart thumps erratically as I watch Sam slowly slide down to sit in the middle of the sidewalk. People step around her and cast puzzling looks down at her, which I answer with a simmering glare of my own.

"Sir, I think it would be best if I spoke to Samantha about that," The woman says.

"Grace, right? That's what she said your name is. Well, Grace, whatever you said to her has her in a borderline catatonic state. So, why don't you tell me what the hell you told her so that I can help her." My voice is intimidating and aggressive, but right now, I can't find it in me to care. The only thing that matters is figuring out how to help Sam.

"I told her that I worked with her parents eighteen years ago to bring her home. They went through an agency in Atlanta, and I was their point of contact," she pauses before finishing, her words already piecing the pieces together in my mind. "She's adopted, Ryan."

"Shit," I whisper as I take in the petite blonde sitting cris-cross on the sidewalk in front of me. Her usually tan skin is more akin to that of a ghost now, and her fingers tremble in her lap. I don't know how much of a shitstorm one person can take before they lose their marbles, but I think Sam might be right on the precipice of cracking.

"I know she mentioned her dad passed, but what about her adoptive mom?" Grace asks kindly. I sigh before responding.

"She passed from cancer about five months ago. Both her parents are gone now," I say, and my fingers tighten around the phone. This isn't fucking fair. Sam doesn't deserve this, and her parents should still be here. It's all bullshit.

"I'm so sorry to hear that," Grace states solemnly. "Look, I can find the information that was on file for the birth parents listed during the adoption and forward them to this number if Sam would like the opportunity to know more about herself. She can always decide to delete the information if she doesn't want it—either option is completely hers to make."

"I appreciate that. Look, I need to go, but thank you for your time, Grace." I hang up and slide Sam's phone into my back pocket. Then, I bend down and pick her small frame up off the concrete. She just shuffles closer to my chest as I carry her to my truck. I open the door and sit her in the passenger seat. Pulling the buckle across her chest, I say, "Let's get you home."

She snorts softly, the first sign of life that she's shown in a while and whispers, "I don't have a home." My heart constricts, but I don't know the right thing to say right now. All I can do is get in the truck and drive us to the privacy of her home.

A short time later, I park in the driveway. The whole drive home, she said nothing. If she weren't blinking and breathing at regular intervals, I would be taking her straight to a hospital. I cut the truck off and sit in the silence for another moment before speaking.

"Do you want to talk about it?" I ask. It sounds like a dumb question and the bare minimum of a conversation starter in this situation, but I'm in uncharted territories here.

Sam just stares ahead at her house as if the answer to all her questions will walk right out the front door at any moment.

"How could they keep that from me?" She asks softly. She still doesn't look my way, but I can see the tears gathering in her eyes.

"Maybe they just never found the right time," I try to justify. Mark and Rose were always two of the kindest and most loving people in my life. I know they would never have set out to intentionally hurt their daughter, and no matter what anyone says, Sam was their daughter. The lack of resemblance between Sam and her parents and their completely polar opposite personalities is starting to make a lot of sense, though.

"The right time?" Sam finally turns to look at me, and there's a new fire in her eyes that's been missing since I found her on that bedroom floor yesterday. "They had eighteen years, Ryan!"

"I know, but I can't imagine it was an easy topic to bring up to a child. They were doing their best, and they always intended to tell you. The lockbox was proof of that."

"Of course you would defend them," Sam scoffs.

"What the hell is that supposed to mean?" I ask, our usual animosity rearing its head again. Sam rolls her eyes and laughs harshly.

"You always had your head up their assess, and they just couldn't get enough of you. It was always 'Ryan, Ryan, Ryan,' and I was left feeling like the outsider in my own home. You have your own parents, Ryan. Why did you have to come along and take mine, too?"

"You don't know what you're talking about, Sam," I say sharply. I know her emotions are running high right now, but I'm not going to sit here and listen to her shit on her amazing parents just because they had one big fuck up.

"No, I have to know," she pushes. "What made them so much more special than your own parents, huh? Was it the way they doted on you like the long-lost son they never had? What, did they have to offer that you couldn't get at your own damn house?"

"They were fucking normal, Sam!" I yell, my anger at her insolence bubbling over. She's always been so goddamn blind to the people around her. "They were kind and loving, and they didn't drink themselves into a coma on the sofa each night like my mom. And they sure as hell never beat me like my dad. Your parents were my safe space, but you were too blinded by your hatred for me to realize that they were always your safe space, too," I finish with an exasperated breath. My hands shake with rage, and I grip the steering wheel until my knuckles turn white.

Sam looks at me now with shocked sympathy etching its way onto her face, and I hate that look. I want to wipe it away and go back to her yelling about how much she hates me. I don't need her pity.

"Here," I say as I let go of the steering wheel to grab her phone out of my pocket and toss it to her. "Grace said she'd send you the details on how to locate your birth parents. You know, in case there's another person out there that you want to take for granted until their last breath." The words tumble out of me before I can process their potential damage.

The sympathy falls off Sam's face, fury replacing it. Her eyes shimmer with angry tears as she grasps the door handle and rips it open.

"Go to hell, Ryan," she snarls, climbing out and slamming the door hard enough to shake the truck. I watch as she angrily walks to the front door, unlocks it, and safely enters. Putting my truck into reverse, I move to the next driveway over and park. The carcass of a home greets me as the memories of my childhood threaten to consume me.

"I'm already in hell, Sam," I mutter as I exit the truck and head into the lion's den.

Chapter Nine

Sam

My life is a cosmic joke. I've concluded that I fucked up so royally in one of my past lives that I'm being punished for it again and again in this one.

I absentmindedly stir the noodles into the boiling water as I stare out the kitchen window. It's been a few hours since Ryan dropped me off, and the evening sun sets in splashes of orange and pink over the trees. Grey-blue eyes plague my thoughts, sending a wave of self-loathing cascading through me. I saw Ryan nearly every day growing up, and I never once suspected such upheaval in his home life. I mean, yes, his parents were odd and anti-social, but I never considered that they could be abusive or dangerous. I didn't question it when he broke his arm and said it happened during football practice or when he came to dinner with a black eye and busted lip after supposedly roughhousing too hard. He then proceeded to shovel down three plates of food as if he hadn't eaten in days.

It all seemed normal to me then, a boy who played sports and roughhoused with friends showing up with bruises and broken bones. All the signs were there, and yet, I couldn't see it. Did my parents know? Perhaps they suspected something, but there's no way they would have left him there with his parents if they knew the truth.

God, he must have been so scared. *"But he felt safe here,"* I think, and that self-hatred turns to acid in my throat. The kind and thoughtful boy next door was constantly terrified and in pain. He came here for years to find safety and love, and I made it a hostile environment at every turn. A sudden wave of gratitude washes over me as I think of all the love and warmth my parents showered me with over the years. I refused to let myself feel and appreciate that love all because the dark fog in my mind told me that it wasn't real; that I wasn't enough and would never be enough.

Ryan's words from our fight in the truck replay in my head on repeat. He's right—I spent so long focused on all the attention and love that my parents gave Ryan that I never took the time to appreciate all that they gave me.

"But they never gave you the truth," My thoughts supply, pushing forward the revelations of today that I've been shoving to the back of my mind for the past few hours. I stir the pasta again and turn to look at the old polaroid sitting on the counter. It's a sepia tinged shot of a young woman with long golden waves, high cheekbones, and full lips holding an infant in her arms. The baby is wrapped in a white blanket with yellow daisies on it and looks at the young girl with complete adoration. The similarities between the woman in the photo and the reflection that stares back at me in the mirror are glaringly obvious. However, I refuse to acknowledge that truth. How can I sit here and give a stranger the title of being my birth mother? She's nameless, and up until today, she didn't exist.

"And she gave you up," my brain reminds me. That thought feeds the dark fog that lives inside my mind. She didn't want me, and she discarded like the piece of trash I've always felt like. No matter what her story was, if she had truly loved and

wanted me, she would have fought to raise me. But then again, I wouldn't have wanted me either. Perhaps she dodged a bullet by passing me off like the curse that I am.

My spiraling is suddenly interrupted by the sound of water splashing onto the hot stove. The boiling pasta water overflows, sending noodles toppling over the edge.

"Shit!" I exclaim as I rush forward and grab the pot handle, pulling it off the eye. Scorching water splashes onto my skin, and I hiss in pain. That familiar feeling creeps in, though, turning the searing pain into a grounding comfort. That familiar vibration of release spreads through me, and I inch my hand back closer to the pot. Balling my hand into a fist, I press the inside of my wrist flush against the side of the pot. I cry out as the pain laces up my arm. Biting my lip, I force myself to keep my wrist against the hot metal. This pain is the most release I've gotten, and no thoughts fill my head in this moment. There's only exquisite pain.

When the buzzing in my brain starts to fade and throbbing pain begins to set in, I pull my wrist back. The assaulted skin is red, raw, and immediately starts to bubble. It's more damage than I've ever done to myself, and my stomach rolls a little. Crying out, I grab the handle and throw the full pot into the sink. I cut off the stove and sink to the floor. Sobs wrack my body as disgust with myself floods my system.

"It's no wonder she didn't want you," The fog in my brain supplies. *"Who would want such a mess?"*

"No one," I whisper to the empty kitchen. The silence of the house and the truth in my words settle deep in my bones. I've never felt so alone.

I don't know how long I sit there before a loud dinging echoes through the house, startling me. I force my shaking legs to stand and realize just how much time has passed. The previously orange and pink sky has turned various shades of black and blue outside of the kitchen window. The dinging sounds again, and I realize that it's coming from the doorbell. Looking down at my injured wrist, I curse, grab a towel off the counter, and lay it casually over my wrist and hand. The touch stings, and I bite my gum to keep the look of pain off my face.

Making my way to the front door, I open it to find Ryan standing on the porch. He's changed since earlier, now sporting a pair of black gym shorts and a grey shirt. He holds up a box of pizza and smiles casually.

"I figured you might be hungry," he says. "Unless I'm too late?" Ryan nods to the dish towel draped over my wrist and hand that holds the edge of the door.

"Uh, no. No, I haven't eaten," I stammer, completely perplexed by his relaxed demeanor. It's as if the conversation in the truck from just hours ago was a figment of my imagination. I must be staring at him as though I've lost my mind, because he raises an eyebrow and lifts the pizza box higher.

"So, can I come in, or would you prefer I take the bedroom window route?" He winks, and I shake my head with a surprisingly genuine laugh.

"You're insufferable," I tell him as I step aside and invite him in. The smell of cheese and pepperoni fills the air, and my stomach grumbles viciously. Have I even eaten today? The sudden stabbing pain in my stomach reminds me that I haven't, and my feeble attempts at dinner earlier ended in disaster. My wrist throbs at the recent memory, and I reposition the towel to look as least awkward as possible.

Ryan sets the pizza on the counter and moves to the cabinet to grab plates. The fact that he knows where everything is in the house doesn't surprise me, but the ease with which he occupies this space does. Even without Mom or Dad here, he still seems comfortable. I doubt I would feel the same way in his home.

"You've never even seen his home," I remind myself. *"You've always been too selfish to even try and know him."* That familiar feeling

of guilt resurfaces, and I try to push it away as Ryan places two slices of pizza on a plate and hands it to me. *"Maybe we can start over, and I can do better this time,"* I think as I take my plate to the barstool and sit at the kitchen island.

I smile at Ryan as he loads three slices onto his plate and closes the box. He moves around the counter until he's standing at the stool next to mine. I reach out to pull the stool back in an invitation for him to sit, but I forget about the damn towel on my wrist. It falls to the floor, and I hear the moment Ryan sees the damage. A gasp leaves his lips, and he sets his plate on the counter before reaching out and grabbing my arm in a gentle grasp.

"Sam, what happened?" Ryan asks, his tone dangerously deep. He turns my arm over in his hand to inspect for any other injuries but finds none. I try to pull my arm back, but his large hand easily holds me in place.

"It's nothing, Ryan. I was trying to cook and had an accident. That's all," I explain, nodding my head to the discarded pot of water and pasta in the sink. It's not really a lie, more like a half-truth. I try to school my expression, but Ryan seems to see right through it.

His eyebrows furrow as his fingers ghost over the fresh burn. "This looks a little more severe than just a cooking accident, Sam." There's an accusation to his statement, but I can tell he isn't going to come straight out and say it.

I swallow, trying to find a way out of this conversation and the words that will wipes away his suspicions. His beautiful eyes bore into me as if trying to pull the truth out of me. I refuse to let him see the real version of me; I'm too close to the edge of the abyss, and I cannot pull him down with me.

"It was already bad when it first happened, then I put ice on it, which apparently you aren't supposed to do," I lie with a nervous laugh. Ryan huffs in disbelief and shakes his head. He drops my arm gently and take his seat next to me.

"No wonder Mark always did all the cooking around here," He jokes. I don't laugh this time, but I'm at least grateful that he's dropping the topic. His eyes, however, still glance at my wrist and back at the pot in the sink as if he's piecing a puzzle together.

We both sit and eat in silence for a few minutes before Ryan pulls out his phone and starts typing on it. A moment later, soft music begins to play from his phone speaker. The ambience puts me at ease, and I realize that this might be the first time I've ever enjoyed Ryan's presence. Sitting here with him, eating pizza and listening to soft pop music, I start to feel like maybe I'm not so alone.

Chapter Ten

Ryan

Sam is quiet as she eats her pizza, but there's more color to her cheeks now than I've seen all day. After walking in my house to find my mother gone for the night, I wasted away in my room while scrolling TikTok for a couple hours. Occasionally, I would glance across the way at Sam's window to find the room empty and eventually dark. Not being able to lay eyes on her and know that she was okay after the last forty-eight hours didn't sit well with me.

So, I ordered a pizza and showed up on her doorstep. Forward? Maybe, but at least I didn't break in through the window.

Alarm bells have been ringing in my head since Sam opened the door with a towel draped across her wrist. Her eyes were bloodshot and even puffier than they'd been earlier. When the towel fell from her arm and I saw the gruesome burn on her wrist, I wanted to yank her off that stool, press her into the safety of my arms, and never let go. She's hurting in a way I don't know how to approach. She said it was an accident, but I'm not sure I buy that explanation. Either way, I'm not pushing it tonight. No, tonight, I just want to be in this house with her and make sure she knows she isn't alone.

If I push too hard, she will throw that cold wall of bitterness back up between us, and I won't stand a chance at helping her.

"I'm sorry," Sam says softly. My hands pause midair holding the plate I was putting in the sink. I turn my head to look at her in disbelief.

"Was that—an apology, Samantha?" I tease. I set the plate in the sink before turning to give her my full attention. I lean casually against the counter and take in her rigid posture. Her cheeks are flushed, and her eyes dart around to look at anything that isn't me.

"Just let me get this out, okay?" She finally brings her eyes up to meet mine, and the panic in them has my spine straightening.

"I'm sorry for the way I've acted over the years. I was dealing with my own shit and couldn't admit it. Instead, I made everything your fault without even giving you a chance to defend yourself. I vilified your relationship with my parents and cost myself precious time with them. I just—never felt like I fit here. But you came in and fit so perfectly with them. I despised you for it, but I should have been thanking you," Sam states in a rapid river of emotion. Her beautiful blue eyes glisten with tears as she continues.

"You gave them so many wonderful memories when I was too deep in my head to be the child they needed. So, thank you for that." A lone tear escapes her eyes, and she quickly wipes it away. My heart constricts at the insinuation that she wasn't enough; Mark and Rose loved her with every fiber of their being, and I'll be damned if I don't make her see that.

"Sam, you were everything they needed. You were the manifestation of their dreams, not me. I could never have taken your place, and I never wanted to. I just wanted to be... here." I lift my hand to the open space of the house that was always so full of warmth, laughter, compassion, and comfort. "I'm sorry if

I ever made it seem any other way."

Sam nods, and her lip starts to tremble.

"Can you promise me something?" She asks in a broken voice. "Promise me I'll never be alone," she begs, and my heart shatters. A sob leaves her throat, sending tears cascading down her angelic face. I stagger forward and grab her off the barstool, pulling her into my chest. I wrap my arms around her and hold on for dear life.

"I'm right here, Sam, and I'm not going anywhere," I declare. She nods her head against my chest and wraps her arms around my waist. This is the first time we've ever hugged, and it feels like a total eclipse, blacking out the memory of every girl I've touched before now because none of them felt like this. A simple embrace shouldn't feel life-altering, and yet, somehow it does.

"If you ever need a reminder that you aren't alone, just think of the sound of my heartbeat in this moment," I say as I cup her head against my chest. "Because as long as it's still beating, then you're never alone, Sam." I tighten my hold on her, resting my chin on the top of her head. She doesn't respond, but she relaxes in my hold as her tears soak my shirt.

We stay there in that grounding embrace for a while longer before Sam's sniffles turn into even breaths. She pulls away first, and it takes every ounce of my restraint not to haul her back into my arms. She glances around and shuffles uncomfortably on her feet.

"Hey," I attempt to distract her before she can start second-guessing the last twenty minutes of our lives. "Why don't we go put a bandage on that, huh?" I nod to her wrist, which she self-consciously tucks behind her back.

"Yeah, okay," Sam says, exiting the kitchen with me a step behind her. Her long skirt hug her hips as we climb the stairs, and I force myself to look at my shoes instead of the movements of her perfectly round ass.

Thankfully, a minute later, we are seated on the fluffy lilac comforter in her room. White moon and star shaped pillows litter the floor from where she didn't make the bed this morning. The first aid kit is laid out next to us, and Sam bites her lip nervously as she eyes it.

"Here, let me see," I say, motioning for her to give me her wrist. Sam cautiously displays her arm to me, and bile churns in my stomach again. The burn is large and blistering, an angry bubble already protruding the skin. Something isn't right, here; I know that, but I'm too afraid to push the bounds of this newfound rapport. If I say the wrong thing, I'm afraid she will shut down, throw me out, and lock the door for good.

I clench my teeth, jaw ticking painfully, as I bite down the urge to ask for the truth. Instead, I grab the gauze pads and lay a double layered square over the burn. Then I wrap her small wrist in a quick spiral of bandaging and secure it in place.

"Wow, you're quite efficient at bandage work," Sam jokes. She holds up her wrist and inspects my work. "Moonlight as an intruder and a nurse, Ryan?" She asks with a chuckle. I want to laugh, too, because a Sam joke is a rare commodity, but it feels sours in my mouth.

"Nah, I uh, had to fix myself up at lot over the years," I admit with a dejected smile. Sam's eyes widen with understanding. Shame and pity flash across her face, and I desperately want to change the subject, but maybe opening up to Sam will help her feel comfortable enough to do the same.

"Has it stopped?" She asks with a bated breath. I swallow and nod.

"Yeah, once I was big enough to swing back. About two years ago, I decided I was through being my dad's punching bag, and Mom was just too content to let me take the brunt of all his anger to do anything about it," I explain, and the anger at my mother's negligent behavior rears its ugly head. While my dad was a monster, my mom's inability to even try to protect me somehow inflicted the most damage.

"After a brutal beating that caused me to miss a whole month of football, I told myself I was done. The next time he came at me, I was going to swing right back. That night, he came home from work exceptionally pissed," I pause as memories that I've tried so hard to forget start flooding my brain. Closing my eyes, I take a deep breath and feel a soft hand land on mine. I blink to see Sam scooting closer on the bed, her hand clasping mine gently.

"Hey, you're not there anymore," she reassures me. A lock of blonde hair escapes her messy ponytail, and a ferocious need to reach out and tuck it behind her ear overcomes me.

"Yeah, I know," I say softly as I give in to the need to touch her and allow my thumb to gently stroke the side of her hand. "That night, he started picking a fight with me, and I knew it wasn't going to end well. I told him to leave me alone and tried to go up the stairs to my room. He caught me at the foot of the stairs and swung. I went down hard on the steps, and he got a few good kicks in before I could make my move. I kicked my leg out and struck him in the knee. Before he could recover, I stood up and punched him so hard that he just slumped to the floor, unconscious. I ran as fast as I could to my room and locked myself inside. I was terrified of what he would do when he woke up," I admit, the memory of the fear I felt sending a tremor through my body.

"And what did he do?" Sam asks in a low tone, her voice almost a whisper.

"He left," I tell her with a small smile. "When he came to, I heard him slamming cabinets and drawers, yelling about how he wasn't going to live in a house full of disrespectful little pricks. He never came to my room, though, and I stayed locked inside of it until I heard the front door slam shut an hour later. I guess he couldn't handle fighting someone who fights back." My smile widens now as pride glistens in Sam's eyes.

"Mom never forgave me, though, and she only works enough to

keep a roof over our head and alcohol in her system. But it's blue skies ahead, now, because I am getting out of this town," I tell Sam. Not only did I get picked up to play ball for the University of Georgia, but I got a full ride academic scholarship as well. I thought I didn't have anyone in my corner to be proud of me, but then Mark damn near shit his pants when I told him. It was one of the best moments of my life.

A small frown forms on Sam's petite face, and my brows crease.

"What's wrong?"

"Nothing. It's just—I applied to UGA as well for their art program, but I got waitlisted," she says, and my heart stutters. I've been struggling with the idea of moving away from Sam, but the idea that she could end up in the same place as me sends a spark of electricity through me.

"Well, that's not a no," I tell her optimistically. Hell, I'll bend over backwards and sell my soul to the admissions board if it means they'll let her in. She smiles, and it quickly turns into a yawn.

"I guess that's my cue," I state as I stand and begin closing the first aid kit. Sam reaches out and grabs my forearm, halting my movements.

"You're coming tomorrow, right?" Sam asks me, referring to Mark's service. The idea of not going never even crossed my mind.

"Of course," I say. "I wouldn't miss it for the world." I give her my best smile before moving to the window. I grab the edge of it and pull up. Sure enough, it doesn't resist my touch and glides open.

"Tisk tisk, Samantha. What have I told you?" I chide. Sam rushes over, her skirt rustling in the night air.

"What are you doing? Use the front door, you animal!"

I laugh at her astonished expression as I throw one leg out the window.

"And where would be the fun in that?" I wink, and Sam's plump lips part in an inadvertently seductive manner. A chuckle leaves me as I climb the rest of the way out the window and down the tree.

"You're going to break your damn neck one day!" Sam yells out her still open window. I turn to look back at her and grin.

"For you, it's worth the risk," I declare. A buzzing energy fills my body as I jog across the yard to my house, leaving Sam to gape at my retreating form. Beneath her gaze and the glow of the moonlight, I've never felt more alive.

Chapter Eleven

Sam

Death is an all-consuming insatiable beast. It doesn't just drain the soul of one person and leave with its spoils of victory. No, death lingers, slowly eating away at the life force of the living left behind to clean up the bloodshed.

I see its damage in the faces surrounding me as we crowd into the small funeral home. My father's work colleagues and friends line the pews, and vibrant floral arrangements take up every inch of space around the white casket at the front of the room.

My father's body lays in the plush-lined casket, clothed in his favorite worn green t-shirt, faded jeans and socks. No shoes, because he absolutely would haunt my ass if I sent him to the grave wearing sneakers.

I stand back at the front row and watch as people come up one by one to say their goodbyes to my father. Many come over to me and offer their condolences, and I try my best to engage in small conversations with each of them. My responses feel forced as grief numbs my body. Ryan stands next to me dressed in black slacks and a white button down, his bicep and chest muscles straining against the silk fabric with each movement.

I'm going to hell for even noticing that right now.

My cotton black dress with short sleeves and knee-length skirt feels itchy and suffocating against my skin. I should have burned this cursed thing after mom's funeral. I never wanted to wear it again, but for some reason, I couldn't bring myself to part with the dress I'd been wearing when I watched her casket be lowered into the ground.

Pulling it out of my closet this morning felt like a bitch slap to the face.

I self-consciously rub at the bandage on my wrist as more people make their way through the viewing line. A few eyes linger on the bandage as they pass me, but no one's brave enough to say anything.

Eventually, everyone takes their seats, and a hushed silence falls over the room. My dad was a very loved and cherished person if the filled pews and wall of standing visitors is anything to go by. He may not have had much family outside of me and Mom, but he sure as hell had a lot of friends. It's cliché to say that someone who passed was very loved and lit up every room they walked into, but it would be the truth for my dad. It's not something anyone would say at my funeral, and the pews surely wouldn't be as filled as they are today.

It feels surreal to be back here again, but this time, without Dad by my side. I tried before everyone arrived to go up and see him one last time, but the memory of my mom's cold, stone-like body lying in a casket bombarded my brain. She had looked unrecognizable, and not just because of the cancer that had eaten away at her. No, there was something in the waxiness of her skin and stiffness of her body that haunted me. I'm not sure I can survive seeing my dad like that, too.

Ryan shifts in the seat next to me as the preacher begins the service. I glance at him as he wipes his palms on his pants. I remember his same rigid posture sitting on the other side of my father at mom's funeral months ago. Back then, I found his presence unnecessary and enraging. Now, I find it alarmingly comforting. I grip my fingers together tightly and resist the urge to reach over and touch his hand. The need to give him the same comfort that he's given me the past couple of days is suddenly overwhelming.

I force myself to focus on the preacher's words as he speaks about my father and then turns the service into a sermon of sorts. My mother's funeral was the same way, and while I've never been a religious person, it was something they both wanted incorporated into their services. Sometime later, the preacher finishes his part and moves on to the moment I've been dreading.

"Now, Mark's daughter would like to say a few words about her father if you would so kindly give her your attention." He moves back from the podium and motions for me to take his place. I force myself to stand on shaking legs and try to take a step forward, but terror roots me in place. Denial slams into me with the force of a freight train. This can't be real. I can't possibly be here doing this again. I'm stuck in some lucid nightmare that I can't wake up from, that's the only explanation.

My heart thumps erratically as the people around me turn to look my way. I glance at the casket and the podium standing on the altar above it, and black spots dance in my vision. My breaths come in shorter pants, and I'm on the verge of passing out when a large hand wraps around my own.

Ryan stands, interlocking his fingers in mine and gives my hand a warm squeeze. His small smile causes a few of the black spots in my vision to recede, and I try to focus on the little dimple on his left cheek.

"Come on, you've got this," he whispers in my ear before taking the first step toward the podium. I take a steadying breath and finally force my legs to follow him. As we climb the steps to the altar, I tighten my grip on Ryan's hand until I'm scared it will bruise. He doesn't seem to mind, just leads me to the podium and then moves to stand beside me. His hand doesn't release mine, and I find myself pulling strength from his grip as I search for my words.

"My dad had a magnetic soul," I begin, my voice shaking with emotions. "He wasn't someone you could meet just once and be okay with never seeing again. He had the kind of laugh that could spread warmth through your veins, and a smile that could banish the darkest of shadows." I pause as I grip the edge of the podium, my other hand draining the circulation out of Ryan's.

"He was a force of life who just wanted to help others feel better, whether that be through his ridiculous jokes, words of wisdom, or his delicious cooking." Many people in the pews nod and smile, their memories of my father being pulled to the forefront of their minds.

"The last few months, however, his jokes happened less often, and more takeout boxes filled the kitchen trash can. Not because he no longer wanted to help lift people up, but because he was now the one who needed lifting. The one person who could do that, however, had already left this earth." My words tumble past trembling lips as I look over all the somber faces staring back at me. The truth settles deep in my bones as I remember the way my father looked when the hospice nurse announced my mother's time of death. He may not have left this earth that day, but it was certainly the day his life started to end.

"While it is heartbreaking for us to be here today and be the ones left to say goodbye, I am grateful that I can stand up here and tell you that my father no longer needs lifting. He just needs us to find enough strength to lay him to rest next to the love of his life so that their spirits can slow dance to Conway Twitty in a field of lavender for eternity."

The image of my mother and father wrapped in each other's arms in an afterlife of flowers and sunshine clouds my vision.

Many people wipe their eyes and nod in agreement as I turn to Ryan.

"Thank you," I whisper softly. He nods stiffly with glistening eyes before leading us back down the steps and to our seats. The preacher approaches the podium again and speaks.

"Such beautiful words, Samantha," he states. He goes on to say his final parting messages and instructs everyone to exit the funeral home and proceed to the graveside service. Ryan and I stay seated until everybody has left except for the workers who will move my father to the cemetery.

"Are you ready?" Ryan softly asks me, and I shake my head.

"Not yet," I say as I stand, my legs feeling unsteady atop my black heels. The casket remains open as the workers stand around it waiting on us to leave. As much as I don't want to be haunted by the image of my father in a casket, I know I can't leave here without seeing his face one more time.

"Can I have just a moment, please?" I ask them nervously. They nod with understanding and move to stand a few feet away. I walk up to the casket and feel Ryan's large presence following me.

My father's still body comes into view, and a wave of dizziness sweeps through me. I cautiously touch the side of the casket to steady myself and look down at his frozen form. His hands lay crossed at his chest like they would be when he'd fall asleep in the recliner watching football. On those days, I would laugh softly before grabbing a blanket and laying it across him. Before I would leave, though, I would always press a single kiss to his forehead.

Time stands still now as I reach a trembling hand out and gently push the strands of brown hair off his forehead. The cold skin that greets my fingers casts a chill into my body that travels through my veins and into my heart.

"I'm so sorry, Daddy," I whisper brokenly. "I love you."

I lean forward and press my quivering lips to his forehead, my tears falling into his hair. I linger there for a moment before moving back and nodding to the workers.

"Are you okay?" Ryan asks as I move towards the exit. I shake my head, and that familiar fog creeps into my brain.

"Hey," Ryan gently grabs my elbow, halting my steps. "You're not alone, remember?" His grey-blue eyes look at me intensely as if trying to vanquish the fog that I know he can't possibly see.

"I know, thank you," I say softly. We walk through the doors of the funeral home just as the lid closes on my father's casket, the sound echoing in the chambers of my heart.

Chapter Twelve

Ryan

Hours after the service, Sam and I sit on the sofa in her living room, a half-eaten casserole sitting on the coffee table in front of us. There's three more just like it stacked in the fridge from the moms in the neighborhood who are kind enough to make sure Sam doesn't starve. I think if I hadn't been here to mentally count each bite that she took, she would have just chucked them all in the trash.

There's a familiar look of vacancy making its way into her eyes. She didn't say much at the graveside, just bit her lip so aggressively while watching her father be lowered into the grave that I thought it might bleed. After I drove us home, she silently exited the truck and walked inside. I quickly went over to my house to change into sweats and a t-shirt before heading back over. When I got to her doorstep, a few of the neighborhood ladies were there with arms full of disposable pans.

I carried the food inside and listened for any sound of Sam as I started up a fresh pot of coffee. A few minutes later, Sam came down the stairs dressed in pink pajama shorts and a white shirt with a blue grumpy care-bear on it. She barely acknowledged me standing in the kitchen before she went to sit on the sofa. I brought one of the trays over, setting the whole thing on the coffee table, and handed her a fork.

"Eat," I commanded, leaving no room for debate. She didn't fight me on it, and I found myself relaxing more with each bite she took.

Now, we sit in a surprisingly comfortable silence, sipping hot coffee and watching a rerun of The Office. Sam's snuggled into a fuzzy yellow blanket, her phone sitting on the cushion next to her. Her eyes keep trailing from the television to her phone as if she's waiting on a call. She worries at her lip, and her finger taps mindlessly against her mug.

"What's up?" I ask her. She looks at me with a confused expression, her messy bun of waves bouncing as she tilts her head at me.

"Your phone," I nod to the device. "You keep looking at it like it's going to grow teeth and bite you."

Sam lets out a frustrated breath. "Oh, Grace messaged me last night, but I haven't opened it. I keep looking at my phone, knowing that the information about my birth parents could be right at my fingertips, but I just don't know if I can do it."

I stare at her for a moment, just taking in her beauty. Her little button nose, full lips, high cheekbones, and wide blue eyes are strikingly like those of the woman in the polaroid. She's so effortlessly beautiful, it's a wonder every guy in school never asked her out. I suppose the looks of pure intimidation that I gave every dumbass who looked her way may have had some persuasion. It's not my fault they were too chickenshit to do anything. Well, everyone except Derek.

"Why do you think your dad left that photo for you?" I ask. "I mean, he could have hidden it or thrown it away, but he made sure you would find it and Grace's number along with it. He wanted you to know the truth," I explain. Sam eyes me with apprehension before glancing at her phone again.

"Look, it's completely your choice, but I think your parents wanted you to know who you are and where you came from. I don't think you would be insulting their memory by trying to find those answers. If anything, I think it would give you a better understanding of how they became your parents. It's their story, too." As I finish, a spark of energy flashes in Sam's eyes.

"She must have met them, right? My birth mother, I mean. Do you think they took that photo of her holding me? Do you think she placed me in their arms after that picture was taken and knew that they would keep me safe?" Sam fires her questions off rapidly, a twinkling in her eyes replacing some of that hauntingly vacant look.

"Maybe if I can just talk to her about it all, she can give me a new piece of them to hold onto, and I can get a few answers of my own," she says hopefully. Sam sets down her coffee, reaches for her phone, and unlocks it. Her eyes scan the screen for a moment before turning to look at me.

"Her name's Annie Mason," she says nervously and whispers the name again as if testing to see how it sounds. "And she lived in Buford, Georgia when the adoption took place." That was eighteen years ago, though, and she may not live there anymore. Or be alive for that matter, but I'm not about to say that to Sam.

Sam begins typing on her phone, grabbing the blanket off her lap and throwing it to the side.

"It's a four-and-a-half-hour drive from here," she says without looking up from her phone. "I can do that. I can totally do that, right?" Sam says, finally looking up at me. There's a slight manic look in her eyes, and the sudden shift in energy sets me on edge.

"Yeah, I mean, that's not a bad drive," I tell her, and she nods vigorously before scooting forward to get off the couch.

"Woah, where are you going?" I ask

"To pack a bag," she answers matter-of-factly. I look at my watch and frown.

"You're not seriously leaving on a four-hour drive at 8:30 at night, are you?"

"Why not?" Sam responds as she goes to stand. The fabric of her shorts slides up her thighs with the movement, and my hand shoots out to grab her knee, halting her in place.

"Sam, what the hell is this?" I ask in shock as my eyes catalog the small oblong scars that litter her inner thighs. There's one that's much fresher than the others, the healing skin a pinkish brown.

"Who did this to you?" My voice cracks as my body registers the truth of what my heart refuses to admit, what I've suspected since watching that towel drop off her wrist. She does this to herself.

Sam's eyes widen, and she tries to move out of my grasp, but I tighten my hold.

"Who did this, Sam?" I growl, my fingers flexing against her leg. I've dreamed about feeling the skin of her thighs underneath my fingers, but not like this.

Shivers roll through her body, and she starts to tremble in my touch.

"It's—they're not—," she stammers, tears filling her eyes. "It's the only way, Ryan," she whispers brokenly.

"Like hell it is!" I let go of her leg and stand up, crowding over her. I press my hands into the cushion on either side of her head and lean in close enough to smell the coffee on her shaky breath.

"I don't care what you or anyone else is feeling, no one is allowed to hurt you. Including yourself. Do you understand?" I growl, rage and concern warring against each other inside of me.

Sam's face reddens from embarrassment or anger, I'm not sure which. Her chest heaves in tandem with mine as my words shine a searchlight on the darkest edges of her soul. She pales as she realizes that someone finally sees past her bitter façade and through to the raw pain that lives underneath. I always knew there was more going on with Sam. I just never got close enough to see the truth, until now.

"You don't understand, Ryan. It's—it's just all too much sometimes. When everything feels out of my control, I know the one thing I can control is the pain. It's not hurting anyone else," she finishes softly. Her words ignite the rage in me, unable to fathom why in the hell she would think this isn't hurting anyone.

"It's hurting you," I say through gritted teeth. I'm not dropping this. I can't look away now that I've seen the truth. "And if you're parents were here to see it, it would hurt them, too."

"And seeing you in pain hurts me, too," I think, but I don't say those words out loud. Sam's anger spreads through her body like wildfire, the red in her cheeks creeping down her neck and chest.

"Not doing it would hurt me more!" She screams. "You don't understand, it's the only way to let it out before the darkness completely consumes me!" Sam yells and pushes against my chest with all her strength. I don't budge, and she begins to smack her hands against my chest instead. I hold steady, absorbing her blows until she starts to tire herself out. Her pain is a palpable destructive force that I refuse to let consume her.

"Just leave me the hell alone, Ryan!" She screams. Her palms shake against my chest, and I wrap my hands around her wrist and pull her weight towards me. I pivot to fall back against the sofa, pulling her body on top of my lap. A startled gasp leaves her pout lips, and I pull her wrists to my chest, locking her in place.

"I made you a promise, Samantha. I told you that as long as my heart is beating, then you would never be alone. I'm not one to break my promises, and I sure as hell won't be breaking a promise to you. So, when everything starts to slip out of your control, you feel like you're drowning, and you need something to anchor you here, you call me. I'll come battle those dark waters with you. Do you understand?"

Her bottom lip quivers at my words, and I release one of her wrists to reach out and caress it with my thumb.

"It's okay," I whisper to her gently as I sense the icy wall collapsing inside of her. "It's going to be okay."

A sob breaks free of her body, and Sam collapses into my chest. Her cries vibrate through my bones as I cradle her safely in my arms. Tears burn my eyes, and I try to blink them away as the severity of the situation settles over me. How close have I come to losing her over the years? Just how deep do her wounds go? I hold her against me until her sobs eventually subside into sniffles, and she lifts her tear-streaked face to look at me.

"Thank you," Sam whispers softly. She looks at me now in a way she never has before, but I can't discern what she's thinking. Her lips quiver as her eyes map my face, lingering on my lips. She shifts her hips, and I'm suddenly very aware of how our bodies are positioned. I swallow the lump in my throat and try to change the conversation before I do something stupid like try to kiss her. There's no way that would go over well.

"Now," I reach up and brush a tear off her cheek. "How about we pack our bags, get some rest, and we can hit the road first thing in the morning?"

Sam's brows crinkle in confusion. A laugh bubbles out of me despite the last few minutes.

"You don't seriously think I'm letting you travel all the way to the outskirts of Atlanta to meet a stranger all by yourself?" I scoff at the absurd thought. "Not in this lifetime, Samantha. Not a chance."

Chapter Thirteen

Sam

On Tuesday morning, Ryan and I load our bags into his truck and stop at the local bank to get the card my dad left for me. My fingers feel numb as I slide it into my wallet and climb back into the truck alongside Ryan. It feels icky to think about using my parents' money to go find my birth mother, but Ryan's right. They must have wanted me to do this, otherwise, they wouldn't have left the truth sitting in a box for eighteen years and handed me the key to it upon their deaths.

They could have taken this secret to the grave with them, but they didn't. They gave me a choice, and I choose to honor their journey and do everything I can to learn more about what happened all those years ago. I want to understand just how fate brought them to be my parents.

Ryan puts on a pop playlist and turns on the navigation as he merges us onto the interstate. His black tee and gym shorts shouldn't catch my attention the way that they do, but I can't help but notice the way the thin fabrics accentuate his muscles any time he moves. The backwards baseball cap he pushes over his hair surely shouldn't affect me the way it does, and yet heat gathers between my thighs every time I glance his way.

"In 128 miles, take exit 156," the GPS states, shaking me from my obvious ogling. I gape at the screen and look out at the drab Georgia road.

"Why couldn't there have been a scenic route?" I complain as I kick off my shoes and fold my legs underneath me. I can feel Ryan tracking my movements out of the corner of his eye, and I self-consciously pull at the edge of the black biker shorts that stop at my midthigh. The scars are perfectly covered, but I swear Ryan can see them anytime he looks my way.

Last night still feels like a fever dream. One moment I was convincing myself that this trip needed to happen immediately, and the next, Ryan was boxing me in on the couch and pulling my darkest confession out of my scarred body. Then, he cradled me on his lap and swore he'd fight the darkness with me. No one had ever spoken to me like that, and a warmth rushed through my core at his words.

Now, I'm afraid he will look at me in the light of day and realize just how fragmented I am and run for the hills. Apprehension runs through my veins, and since when do I find the idea of Ryan getting the hell out of my life devastating? A week ago, I would have paid good money to never see him again. Now, I can't stop looking over at him and remembering the way his hands felt wrapped around my wrists last night as he pressed me to his chest and held me in place on his lap.

The position had been intimate, but it hadn't felt awkward. No, it felt right, like I was made to fit perfectly against him.

I've only ever dated one person, Derek, and while we had physically taken our relationship all the way, I never once felt the way that I did when pressed against Ryan's chest last night. I had looked into his eyes and felt a fire in my core that I'd never felt before. While I've always known and admitted that Ryan was handsome, looking at him never made me want to devour him the way that I wanted to when straddling him last night. The feelings were so sudden and overwhelming that I just stared at him in dismay while he looked as if he were trying to decipher my thoughts.

"So, what's the plan if we get up there and the person at this address doesn't know an Annie Mason?" Ryan interrupts my thoughts. I glance over at his relaxed posture, his right hand wrapped casually around the steering wheel. My wrists tingle at the memory of his hands on my skin. God, what is happening to me?

"I don't know," I admit. "It's possible she doesn't live there anymore. I mean, it was eighteen years ago. I suppose we could always ask around about her if that ends up being the case. Someone is bound to know her, right?"

"It's possible," Ryan says, his eyes on the road. "Hopefully, she'll still be living there or at least one of her parents."

My thoughts freeze at his words. My grandparents. Somehow, I hadn't thought of possibly meeting them yet. My dad's parents died before they got me, and my mom's parents lived thousands of miles away and never spoke to her. They didn't even have the decency to show up to her funeral. I never learned the full story about what happened between her and her parents, and I regret never asking her.

The idea of getting a second chance at grandparents is nerve wracking. I mean, they must know I exist. Annie looked around my age in that polaroid, and I doubt she would have been able to keep an entire pregnancy and birth a secret. Unless she also didn't have a relationship with her parents.

"If her parents were around back then, why wouldn't they have stepped in and taken me?" I ask Ryan. He shrugs softly and glances my way.

"Maybe they couldn't take care of another child at the time. They could have been sick or financially unwell. There's only one way for us to get the answer to that question," Ryan says, ever the logical thinker. I nod and distract myself by looking around the interior of the truck. It's nice, with leather seats and a touch screen monitor. My brows crease with puzzlement.

"How do you afford this truck?" I ask. I know Ryan never worked in high school since football took up all his free time. Ryan shifts uncomfortably in his seat and glances at me.

"My dad bought it for my sixteenth birthday just three months before he left. I keep waiting on the day I'll wake up and it will be gone from the yard either by repo or his own hand, but it hasn't happened yet. I guess he's still paying the bill. I don't know if that's because some part of him feels bad for everything he did, or he just doesn't want to fuck up his credit. I tend to believe the latter," Ryan explains with a sad smile. There's an obvious hurt in his voice anytime he speaks of his dad, and I wonder where the asshole is now. Perhaps I can track him down and give him a swift kick to the balls.

"Oh," I say softly, my voice not giving away my violent thoughts. "I'm sorry I brought it up." I don't like making him think of his dad and all the awful memories that must be associated with the prick.

"No, it's okay," Ryan states as he turns and offers me one of his genuine smiles. "You can always ask me anything, Sam."

I feel that warm tingly feeling spreading through me as I take in his angular face and beautiful smile. He's so goddamn handsome, it's infuriating. I turn away from him before I can get too wrapped up in that warm feeling and lean my head against the window.

I must fall asleep because some time later, I groggily open my eyes to find us pulling into a small café parking lot.

"Thought we could grab a bite," Ryan says as he puts the truck in park. The navigation shows that we still have over an hour left, but my stomach growls at the prospect of food. I nod and exit the truck, stretching my arms over my head to shake off some of the sleepiness.

Ryan's eyes catch on the small slip of skin that peeks out from the bottom of my shirt when I lift my arms, and I quickly tug it back down as a blush creeps across his face. He clears his throat and moves to open the café door. Thunder rolls overhead, and I glance up to see dark clouds moving into place above us. A drop of rain lands on my forehead, and I quickly move inside the café before more can come down.

Ryan places his hand on the small of my back as he guides us to a booth. The way that his body constantly gravitates toward mine should feel alarming considering last week I would have slapped him for touching my back. Yet, it feels completely natural and sets butterflies off inside of me.

An older woman in a black apron greets us when we take our seats. The café is nearly vacant as the thunder begins to roll outside.

"Welcome in, my name's Marie, and I'll be taking care of you today," she introduces herself and lays the cutlery and menus on the table. "Just a heads up, we will be closing up shop in about an hour so all our workers and customers can make it home before the storm hits." Marie nods to the large window next to us where we can see the dark clouds moving in. Wind starts to sway the trees that line the parking lot, and the daylight quickly starts to dissipate.

"Oh," I say, pulling my phone out to check the weather app. Sure enough, there's a tornado watch and severe storm warning in effect. "We have about an hour and a half left in our trip. Do you think we can make it there before the storm gets too bad? We're heading north." I'm worried that if I don't go to find my birth mother right now, I might talk myself out of it by tomorrow.

"Not a chance, sweetheart," Marie answers kindly. "There's already been a few tornado outbreaks two towns over, and the storm's headed straight for us. Lucky for you, there's a little motel about two minutes from here. Other than that, there's a few bigger hotels a couple exits up, but you may not get there before the weather picks up."

I look at Ryan who stares back at me with a charming grin.

"It's fine, Sam. It's one night, and then we can hit the road again in the morning. It's just a few more hours we get to spend together." He winks, and I just roll my eyes, refusing to acknowledge that hot feeling that rushes through my body.

"Okay, Marie. I guess we will be staying here, then," I say with a smile. We both order cheeseburgers and fries, eyeing the clouds while we wait on our order.

"So how come you were waitlisted?" Ryan asks suddenly. I pull my gaze from the storm clouds to give him an irritated look.

"What? Why would you even bring that up?" I question. The last thing I need right now is another reminder of my shortcomings. Ryan at least has the decency to look embarrassed as he shakes his head.

"No, I don't mean it like that. I mean, what did your portfolio look like that you submitted? Because there's no way in hell that they saw the same sketches I've seen and still put you on the waitlist." He gives me a knowing look, and I'm reminded of the awestruck expression he wore the night he found my most personal drawing. I had sketched a young woman standing on the shores preparing to be washed away by the destructive wave in front of her. It was a portrayal of my own inner turmoil, of the darkness that threatens to drown me day in and day out. It's certainly not a sketch that I submitted alongside my application.

I shake my head as Ryan once again gets to see a piece of me that no one else has.

"I just gave them what I thought they'd want; sketched flowers, landscapes, stuff like that. I didn't have the best GPA, so I'm not surprised that I ended up on the waitlist," I explain, and Ryan scoffs.

"Come on, Sam. They probably see a thousand sketched flowers a year. What they don't see often is the raw emotion and hyperrealism that accompanies your art. If they saw the real you, they'd never let you go." His words electrify me, and I have to bite my cheek to keep the tears from springing to my eyes.

"I'm just saying, you should reach back out to the department head and send them some of your real work, not the cookie cutter versions you think they want to see. Let them see the real you, Sam. She's a sight to behold," Ryan states, his voice deepening with emotion, and my breath catches in my chest. The way he's looking at me makes me feel stripped bare.

"Here we go." Marie's voice breaks through the lustful haze as she sets our plates on the table. I let out a breath and thank her before dousing my fries in mustard.

"That's revolting," Ryan says as he squirts ketchup over his. I laugh as I pick up a few mustard-covered fries and make a show of moaning as I shove them into my mouth. Ryan nearly chokes on his own fry, and Marie rushes over to pat him on the back as he chugs his water. She stares at me in confusion as I laugh so hard tears form in the corner of my eyes. Ryan just blushes as he gathers his bearings and thanks Marie. She scurries off, reminding us of the incoming storm, and we make quick work of our meals.

After we eat, I pay the bill despite Ryan's protests. There's no way in hell I'm letting him pay for anything during this trip after he dropped everything to drive me up here in search of my unknown origin. We climb back into the truck and follow Marie's simple directions to the nearby motel. The rain is already coming down hard when we park and grab our bags. We haul ass across the parking lot to the front door, and I shriek at the onslaught of rain while Ryan's laughs hypnotically.

Once inside, we are thoroughly soaked and shivering under the motel air conditioning. My shirt clings to my chest, and the guy at the front desk averts his eyes from me under Ryan's intense stare.

"Welcome in," he greets. "How can I help you today?"

"Room for two, please," I respond, placing my card and ID on the counter. My teeth nearly chatter as the AC bombards me.

"You're in luck. We've got one room left, and it's all yours for the night." He grabs the card and scans it before pulling out a keycard. He hands me the items and instructs us on how to get to our room.

"Thank you," I say, and Ryan grabs our bags as I lead us down the hall.

We quickly locate the room in the small motel, and I scan the card to open the door. I follow Ryan in and watch as he places our bags on the floor. He turns to look at the rest of the room, and his eyes widen slightly. I follow his gaze and swallow thickly.

"Why is there only one bed?" I ask nervously. Ryan laughs and moves to stand next to the bed.

"Don't worry, Samantha. I can be a perfect gentleman," he says before pulling his wet shirt over his head.

My jaw drops as my eyes track the large expanse of his shoulders, chest, and chiseled abs. The warm feeling inside of me that only he can cause turns into absolute lava.

Shit, I'm in so much trouble.

Chapter Fourteen

Ryan

I wish I could freeze time and etch every detail of Sam's face in this moment into my mind forever. Her blue eyes widen as they take in the expanse of my naked torso, and my self-confidence skyrockets. I've always been comfortable with my body; spending hours on the football field and lifting weights has its benefits. But the way Sam's looking at me right now is certainly going straight to my head. I casually flex the muscles in my chest and give her a cocky grin.

"What are you—what are you doing?" She stammers nervously. A robust laugh vibrates through me at the absolute panic in her eyes. Her shirt clings to her chest, giving me a tantalizing view of the perky roundness of her breasts. She doesn't seem to notice though as her panicked breathing pushes her breasts against the wet fabric. A shiver runs through her body, and I force myself to break the spell I'm under.

"I'm freezing, Sam," I say as I move away from the bed and to my suitcase. I bend down and grab a fresh pair of sweats and a red t-shirt before heading toward the bathroom. I turn back to see Sam still frozen in place, staring at me in disbelief.

"I'm going to take a shower and warm up. I suggest you do the same. After me, of course," I wink and watch with a grin as pink spreads across her cheeks, and I just can't help myself. "Unless you want to conserve water?" I wiggle my eyebrows suggestively and bellow a deep chuckle when Sam's eyes nearly pop out of her skull. I leave her standing there gaping and let my laughter carry me into the bathroom.

I turn on the shower and strip off the rest of my wet clothes. As I step under the hot water, I can't help but think of Sam standing just outside the door, her clothes clinging to her body. I'm thrown back to the feeling of how her body felt pressed against mine as she straddled my hips while I gripped her wrists in my hands. I start to grow hard as I imagine her grinding against my cock, her plump lips parting in ecstasy. What would it feel like to have those lips pressed against mine, to see them wrapped around my cock?

I force myself out of those thoughts as I turn the shower knob from hot to cold and let the icy water cool my veins and throbbing dick. After composing myself, I dress and exit the bathroom to find Sam sitting on the edge of the bed. Her posture is rigid, and she looks wild with her blonde waves half wet and frizzy. Her obvious discomfort makes me more nervous than the black sky and rolling thunder outside. Shame washes over me at the fact that I was just fantasizing about her in the shower while she sat out here panicked and shivering.

"Hey, I can sleep on the floor tonight. Don't sweat it," I tell her, trying to put her at ease. As much as I love to pester her, I would never want to intentionally make her uncomfortable. She blinks at me and shakes her head.

"No, that's ridiculous. You're not sleeping on the floor, Ryan," she huffs out my name, seemingly agitated with my offer.

"Okay...," I say, stressing the single syllable word. I scratch my head and glance around anxiously, unsure of how to put her at ease.

"It's just that I don't typically sleep well. I toss and turn for hours most nights. My brain just has a hard time turning off. I don't want to keep you up all night, too." Sam looks embarrassed as she explains, though my brain can't process why that would be embarrassing. I've spent many nights lying in bed haunted by the memories of bruises and broken bones or waiting to see if my dad would break down the door and drag me out of bed over something meaningless.

"Don't worry, Sam. I'm a heavy sleeper," I lie. She just nods and stands before grabbing her clothes and heading to the bathroom. I try to not think about rivulets of hot water cascading down her skin as I hear the shower turn on. Letting out a sigh, I head over to the bed and fluff the pillows. I prop them up against the headboard and then rifle through my suitcase for the few snacks I packed. Once I find what I'm looking for, I grin and walk over to the small microwave sitting in the tiny kitchenette. I put the bag in, and a popping sound and the smell of butter fills the air.

While the popcorn pops, I grab the tv remote and scroll through the limited movie options. The thunder rumbles outside, rain beating against the window. The signal on the tv flickers as I flip through the channels before eventually landing on a winner. The microwave beeps, and I grab the popcorn out and open the bag.

Buttery steam coats my nostrils, the smell and warmth reminding me of the many evenings spent on Mark and Rose's couch shoveling handfuls of popcorn into my mouth while we all watched the latest blockbuster film. I would marvel at the ease and comfort in their routines, and then tiptoe back into my house trying to avoid my father's wrath.

Movie nights with the Millers became my lifeline, something I clung to and counted down the days for. We hadn't had one since Rose got sick, and it was too painful to even bring up after she died. Right now, though, I think Sam and I could both benefit from a sliver of comfort and normalcy.

With no bowl to pour the popcorn in, I take two of the disposable coffee cups off the kitchenette counter and fill both with popcorn. Smiling proudly, I take the cups to the bed and crawl onto one side. I sit against the pillows with my long legs crossed at my ankles and wait for Sam to come out.

A moment later, she exits the bathroom, steam spilling into the bedroom before she closes the door. Her wet hair cascades down her back, and her blue eyes are luminous despite the dim motel lighting.

I've learned over the years that Sam prefers baggy graphic tees and shorts in lieu of typical cutesy pajama sets. Tonight's no different as she comes closer to the bed donning a large Bob Ross tee and black shorts.

Sam eyes the bed where I sit against the pillows, and her gaze lands on the cup of overflowing popcorn that I have propped against her pillows. She raises an eyebrow at me and glances between the two cups.

"What's this?" She asks while looking at the popcorn as if it might bite her.

"Popcorn, obviously. And a movie," I say, nodding to the paused tv screen.

"Popcorn and a movie?" She parrots back as if having a hard time comprehending the situation.

"Yes, Samantha. It's popcorn and a movie. Now, sit your cute little ass down please so we can enjoy at least a few minutes of it before the storm knocks the power out of this place."

Sam's mouth falls open, but she doesn't throw back a witty retort. Instead, she just picks up the cup of popcorn and slides under the covers next to me. Her posture is rigid as she sits back against the pillows.

"Alright, then," she says. "What are we watching?"

I hit play on the remote with a grin, and the face of early 2000s

Robert Downey Jr. fills the screen.

"Tropic Thunder, really?" Sam scoffs, and I cut my eyes at her.

"Tropic Thunder is a classic," I protest. Sam doesn't fight me on it, just smiles softly and begins eating her popcorn. I do the same, and we sit in a comfortable silence as the movie plays and the storm rages on outside. It's a familiar comfort, and the absence of her parents weighs heavy on my heart. I miss them so goddamn much. When Rose died, I tried to hide my devastation as to not make it about myself. She wasn't my mother after all, and Sam already despised me enough. With Mark's death, however, I'm having a harder time keeping the grief at bay.

I know it isn't fair to grieve Mark as if he were my own parent, but I credit a large portion of the person I am today to Mark's guiding presence in my life. Had I not had him next door to teach me how to play football, help me with homework, or show me how to cook my own food, I'm not sure I would have survived.

I really fucking miss him.

Sometime later, Sam shifts closer to me, our cups empty and discarded on the comforter. Lightning flashes illuminate the room occasionally, and strong winds beat against the window. The movie ends just as Sam's head starts to fall against my shoulder. I peer down at her and, once again, just admire her beauty. A few light freckles dot her nose, and her closed eyes make her long lashes bring attention to the high slopes of her cheekbones. Her cute little nose twitches as a strand of hair brushes against it. I reach out and tuck the hair back behind her ear, letting my fingers linger against the curve of her neck.

She is the most effortlessly beautiful being I have ever known. It's not a new thought but a fact I've recognized many times over the years. I've tried dating other girls, knowing that Sam hated my guts and would never give me a chance, but I knew the relationships wouldn't last. I was always up front with every girl I dated, though. I didn't do long-term; it was just a casual thing with physical benefits for both parties. They never argued or demanded more, and for that I was grateful. I wouldn't have been able to give them more because my heart already belonged to the girl next door.

Sam's head rocks a little against my shoulder as the credits roll on the movie. Her even breaths give away her unconscious state, and I shift her gently off my shoulder and onto the pillow. As much as I would love to keep her rested against me, the angle that her head was bent at did not look the least bit comfortable.

Her hair fans out across the pillow, and the smell of her coconut shampoo sends a rush of heat through me. God, I cannot get enough of her. She's rapidly unraveling my restraint and doesn't even know it.

I pull the covers up to her shoulders before turning off the tv and rolling over. While I want desperately to just lay here and stare at her, I know it would only pull me deeper into my obsession with her, and that's just not helpful right now. I listen instead to the beautiful sound of her breathing deeply next to me as I close my eyes and drift to sleep.

Darkness morphs into streaks of sunlight as I slowly blink awake. A warm petite body is curled around my own, and long hair tickles my neck.

Ever so slowly, I look down to see Sam laying against my chest, her hair falling in its trademark waves over my neck and shoulder. Her arm is wrapped around my stomach, and her leg is draped across my waist.

I hold my breath, afraid that any movement will startle her awake and shatter this moment. I know she probably didn't plan to end up wrapped around me, but I can't help but want to lay here and bask in the feel of her warm touch. The golden rays of sunlight paint her skin and bring an angelic glow to her hair. It's as if I've stepped through the gates of heaven and entered the afterlife I've always dreamed of.

Carefully, I lift my hand and bring it up to lightly caress the soft strands of her hair. They glide through my fingers like silk, and the smell of coconut and honey overwhelms my senses. On the third pass of my fingers, Sam's eyes flutter open as her body shifts against mine. My hand pauses as she furrows her brows and blinks slowly. She lifts her head suddenly and looks around the sunlit room before finding my gaze.

"It's morning," she states, confusion etching her face. "I slept the whole night?" Sam asks incredulously. Her expression shifts into one of wonder and relief.

"Uh, yeah," I stammer, wondering if she's registered our obvious cuddling position yet. "It was a pretty intense storm. Makes for great sleep," I say casually despite the rapid thumping of my heart.

Her hand glides across my chest as she blinks at me wondrously. The touch sends shivers through me, and my cock twitches. A beautiful grin breaks out across her face, and she shakes her head.

"Where did you come from, Ryan Hartley?" She says with a look of astonishment.

"Next door," I state jokingly with a shrug. Sam laughs under the glow of the sunlight, and it's the most beautiful sight I've ever seen. I grin as her laugh dies down, and she looks at me with a heated expression that sets fire to my skin and spreads warmth to my core.

And then, Samantha Grace Miller kisses me.

Chapter Fifteen

Sam

Kissing Ryan is like drinking pure sunlight—warm, golden, and powerful enough to set you ablaze. The moment my lips touch his, I know I'll never get enough. I'll burn from the inside out just for him. This heat has been building in me since I straddled his hips two nights ago and let him see the darkest depths of my soul, and I'm on the verge of combusting.

When I woke up this morning, bathed in light and pressed against the hard ridges of Ryan's body, I felt safer and more anchored than I ever have. With the week I've experienced, my mind typically would have refused to shut off. After my mom's death, I didn't sleep more than three hours a night for weeks. I would close my eyes and see her deteriorated body in the casket, my body forcing me to reach out and grasp her ice-cold hand. Then, I'd turn, and another casket would appear next to me, my father's still face staring up at me. I'd wake sweating and gasping for breath, refusing to go back to sleep.

The night of my father's death was the first night of dreamless sleep in months, my body having just show down in the face of overwhelming grief and trauma.

This morning, though, I woke up safely wrapped in a cocoon of body heat and sunshine. It was a euphoric feeling that I wanted to bottle up and save for the rest of my life. I had never felt that way, and I couldn't even think as my body fell into his force field and my lips gravitated towards his.

The impact was cosmic.

Now, I gasp against Ryan's soft lips as his hand cradles the back of my neck and presses me closer into him. He takes the opening and deepens the kiss, sliding his tongue against my own.

Kissing him is like wrapping myself in the finest silks and knowing that no other fabric will ever compare. His lips move against mine in their own language, spelling out my damnation and telling me that I will never be the same.

A deep moan vibrates through Ryan's chest beneath me as his teeth sink into my bottom lip. I gasp from the slight sting of pain as pleasure shoots through my veins. Ryan's hand moves into my hair, and he gives it a rough pull, yanking my head back to expose my neck. His lips leave my mouth and press against my throat, leaving trails of soft kisses down to my collarbone. I move to press closer into his body when my hand brushes against his hard cock. He groans beneath me, and it's like a bucket of ice-cold water being poured over me.

I jump back as if I've been electrocuted and nearly fall off the bed. Ryan shoots up wide-eyed, his lips swollen, and pupils dilated.

"I'm-- I'm so sorry," I stammer, pressing my fingers to my tingling lips.

"I'm not," Ryan states gruffly. He shifts forward onto his knees on the bed and grabs my face in his hands. His beautiful blue-grey eyes stare intently into mine as he speaks. "Don't ever apologize to me for acting on the way you're feeling, as long as it isn't hurting you. Understand?" His thumb caresses my bottom lip, and I shiver under his touch. I just nod, unsure of how to respond.

"There's no way we can just act like that didn't happen, right?" I ask, already knowing that the feel of his lips will still be engraved in my memory when I'm one day lowered into the ground.

"Not a chance, Samantha," Ryan says with a wink. Then, he leans down and presses a kiss to my cheek before getting up and heading into the bathroom. I catch sight of the large tent in his sweatpants as he passes, an obvious sign that he was just as much into that kiss as I was.

How can the boy I grew up next to all these years, who I've hated with every ounce of my being, suddenly be the most constant and comforting force in my life?

"What have I done?" I think as I fall back into the pillows, and Ryan's scent engulfs me. I bring my hands over my face and groan. Large hands suddenly wrap around my ankles and yank me to the edge of the bed. I squeal as Ryan stands over me, and he releases my ankles to hold my face between his hands.

"Get out of your head, Samantha. We're okay." His thumb ghosts over my bottom lip as he towers over me. "Now, let's go meet your birth parents," he states with a composed confidence that I don't feel. I just nod as he releases me, the absence of his touch lingering as I get up to get changed.

An hour later, we are on the road again, the storm having passed during the night. Ryan drives casually as the navigation leads us to Buford, Georgia. Neither of us has mentioned the kiss since leaving the motel, but there's an electric energy surrounding us right now that's hard to ignore.

I never thought there would come a day where I would look at Ryan Hartley and imagine what it might feel like to have the hard ridges of his muscles pressed against my bare skin. Just watching the sun illuminate his dark hair and stormy eyes as he drives leaves me utterly breathless. I'm rapidly approaching a point of no return when it comes to him, and I have no idea what to do about it.

As we near the town, I smooth the edges of my light pink skirt for the hundredth time.

"You look great, Sam," Ryan says without even glancing in my direction. "Quit worrying about what they're going to think. They're damn lucky just to be meeting you," he states with conviction. "And you're not alone, okay? I'm right here." He glances at me then, and the softness in his gaze anchors me.

I can totally do this. Right?

Ryan turns back to the road and leads the truck off the interstate and down a few small backroads. We turn left one last time, and the navigation announces our arrival. A small yellow house sits on a corner lot, its brown fence worn from years of weather. A gravel path leads from the road, through an opening in the fence, and up to the quaint home. Small potted plants line the front porch, and a bird bath sits off to the side with colorful daisies painted on it.

The home has a warm and inviting charm to it, and I can't fathom someone thinking that this place wasn't fit for a child.

We park in the driveway and exit the truck. I take a steadying breath in and tuck my hair behind my ears. My palms prickle with sweat, and I wipe them nervously on my white blouse.

"Hey, you've got this," Ryan says as he comes to stand by my side. His presence brings a comforting strength that I desperately need right now. So, for the second time today, I decide to act on what I need. I reach for his hand and thread my fingers through his, squeezing tightly. He squeezes back, and a ridiculous grin spreads across his face.

I smirk and roll my eyes as I take the first step forward to lead us up the porch steps. We reach the worn white door, and I take another deep breath before raising my fist and knocking. I hold my breath as the seconds tick by until I hear a lock turning on the other side. The door swings open, and a plump older woman with a kind face steps into the doorway. Her silver and white hair is cut short, and her familiar blue eyes are hooded with wrinkles. She's wearing a baggy shirt with Elvis Presley's face on it, faded jeans, and white sneakers. Everything about her is comforting and inviting.

"Hi, how can I--," she begins before her eyes meet mine, and her words stop.

"Oh my god, it's you. It's really you," she whispers. Tears fill her eyes, and then I'm suddenly being pulled into her arms.

"I can't believe it's really you. Welcome home, little daisy," she states softly, and I barely register her words as tears fill my eyes. Taking in a shuttering breath, I wrap my arms around her bigger frame and allow myself to embrace her comforting touch.

She feels like home in a way I can't quantify, and I'd be content to stay in this hug forever with Ryan standing awkwardly to the side. She pulls away before I'm ready, and my heart squeezes. The older woman reaches her wrinkled hand up and touches my cheek in a loving motion. Her skin is so soft and comforting, I find myself leaning slightly into the touch.

"Come on in," she says, stepping back to usher us into the home. "We have so much to discuss, little daisy."

Chapter Sixteen

Sam

Following the older woman into the house, my heart pulses to a dangerous rhythm. The fact that I instantly feel so safe and at ease in her presence is overwhelming and terrifying. I can't bear to get attached to anyone else just to lose them. My chest tightens, and my breathing becomes shallow as anxiety fills my body. Ryan's hand finds my own again as we approach a small grey sofa in the living room. I squeeze his hand and try to calm the panic rising inside of me. Now that I'm here, I'm not sure what to say or even how to introduce myself.

The older woman must sense my unease because she sits in the recliner across from us and smiles kindly before speaking.

"I can't believe you're really here," she begins, her eyes cataloging every inch of my face. "I've hoped for this moment every day for the last eighteen years. I've looked for you in the faces of strangers on the streets, just knowing that I would recognize those eyes as soon as I saw them. You look just like my Annie." Tears fill her eyes, and she shakes her head. "I just hoped that fate would be kind enough to bring you back to me one day."

"I'm sorry. I'm getting ahead of myself. I haven't even gotten your name yet. I'm Dorothy Mason, but you can call me Dot or Maw Maw, if ever one day you feel I've earned that honor," she states, her voice wavering slightly. Her beautifully wrinkled face is a map of memories and emotions that she's experienced over the years, and I find myself yearning to hear her speak about each one.

"My name is Sam," I begin nervously. "Samantha Miller, actually. My parents recently passed and left behind a lockbox with documents pertaining to an adoption that took place eighteen years ago."

"Oh, honey," Dot's eyes water with tears as I continue.

"Your address was listed on the official paperwork for my adoption, and I wasn't sure how else to get answers. I apologize for just showing up like this." I squeeze Ryan's hand tighter as he sits on the sofa next to me. His thumb caresses the back of my hand in grounding strokes.

"Nonsense, my door has been open for you since the day you were carried out of it," Dot says with a somber smile. "I know you must have so many questions, but first I need to apologize," she states as she sits leans forward in the chair, her movements stiff with age.

"I'm so sorry, little daisy, that my daughter and I failed you. Annie had been struggling with her mental health since she was a young teen, and after she had you at eighteen, the dark thoughts inside of her became unbearable." Her words strike a chord in me, the fragmented pieces of me starting to make sense.

"She started self-medicating and leaving you with me for days on end. My health wasn't in the best shape either, and I'd just lost my husband to a stroke. I knew I couldn't be the parent you needed, and my daughter just wasn't in the right headspace to be a mother." A tear falls down Dot's cheek, and she wipes it away with a wrinkled hand.

My heart breaks for her as I think of how lonely she must have felt having lost her husband, feeling her daughter slipping away, and then having to say goodbye to her granddaughter. But I also can't help but wonder what it would have been like to grow up in this quaint home with this woman that radiates warmth and kindness.

"You still had an abundance of warmth and kindness surrounding you growing up. You just couldn't appreciate it then," my brain reminds me. Guilt creeps into my bones as I think of all the times my parents tried to shower me with love, and I'd barely reciprocate it. The darkness in my mind would convince me that it wasn't real, that there was no way they could truly love me the way they claimed. I don't remember feeling like that as a little girl, though. It wasn't until I became a teenager that I started to struggle with my self-worth and the authenticity of the relationships around me.

"When Annie returned one day after a week away, I told her that if she couldn't be a dependable and loving mother, then you deserved one who could be. I contacted the adoption agency in Atlanta, and that's how we met Mark and Rose."

My heart skips a beat at the mention of my parents, and I wait on bated breath for Dot to continue.

"When I placed you in Rose's arms for the first time, I knew that she was meant to be your home. She looked at you with the type of adoration only a mother could convey. And Mark, well, he looked at you like you hung the moon and stars. I knew they would take better care of you than I ever could. Please tell me I was right," she says shakily, and another tear falls down her cheek. She doesn't wipe it away this time, just lets another cascade after it.

My throat tightens as wetness mars my own face, and I nod with conviction.

"You were right," I say brokenly. Ryan releases my hand to put his arm around me and pull me into his side. Dot's attention turns to him then, and she eyes him wearily.

"And who is this young gentleman?" She asks with a sniffle. Ryan releases his hold on me to stand and extend his hand to Dot.

"I'm Ryan Hartley, ma'am. I'm Sam's neighbor," He grins. Dot shakes his hand and slides her gaze from him to me.

"Well, can't say I've ever held hands with my neighbor, though I don't think Gary next door would complain if I did."

I smile at her humor but don't address the obvious question in her statement. Mainly because I don't know how to answer it. I don't really know what Ryan and I are, and now doesn't seem like the greatest time to delve into that conversation.

Ryan just laughs it off as he comes to sit back down next to me. For the first time since coming into the house, I notice the paintings of various sizes that line the walls. They are beautiful and chaotic, a mixture of colors, textures, and strokes. In each painting, however, one thing remains consistent. There's a single daisy painted into each, sometimes bigger and sometimes smaller, but it can be found in each one. Dot's words from earlier ring in my mind, and I look back at her again.

"You called me 'little daisy.' Why is that?" I question. Dot smiles and looks at the paintings on the wall.

"That's what Annie named you when you were born, Daisy Mason. Mark and Rose felt like a fresh start would be best when they adopted you, and we agreed. But Annie and I always spoke of you as our little daisy. You were our flower, out there somewhere growing and becoming more beautiful every day. Annie paints a lot during her manic episodes, and she would always find a way to add a piece of you to her art. We never forgot you, Sam, and I'm so sorry that we couldn't do better by you," Dot says, and a sob escapes her throat.

"I'm so sorry," she says again, holding a hand to her mouth to trap another sob.

I rise off the couch and step forward to fling my arms around her, bending at an awkward angle. She stands to meet my embrace, and tears cascade down my cheeks.

"You did just right by me," I whisper to her.

"Oh, my sweet girl," Dot murmurs as she pulls me tighter into her. The comfort of her embrace is heavenly, and I want to sketch the image of her arms around me on paper and frame it forever.

"Now," Dot says as she reluctantly breaks the hug. "Why don't I put us on a pot of coffee while I tell you a little bit about your mother, hmm?" I wipe my tears and nod. Dot moves down the hall and into the kitchen, while Ryan and I trail behind her.

Family photos line the hall walls, and I stop to inspect each one. I can track Dot through the years, her skin more wrinkled in some photos and smoother in others. In a few frames, she stands with a taller man and a young girl. Then, the photos become just her and her daughter, both their smiles dimmer and faces more worn.

"You look just like her," Ryan says from over my shoulder. "It's no wonder Dot immediately recognized you."

I hum in agreement, completely transfixed on the girl in the photos. The polaroid didn't do our similarities justice; I might as well be her clone.

At the end of the hall, a familiar photo hangs on the wall. I stare in confusion at the image of a newborn baby wrapped in a hospital blanket and lying in a bassinet. The same exact photo hangs on my parents' living room wall. Ryan must notice, too, as he steps closer to inspect it.

"That was the day you were born," Dot says, stepping from the kitchen into the hall.

"My parents have this same photo," I state. My mother never had pictures of her pregnancy with me, of course now I know why. While I always felt the physical differences between my parents and I were odd, I never let myself believe I could be adopted because the proof of my birth to them was hanging right on the wall.

Dot must see the hurt in my face because she steps forward and places her hand on my arm.

"I'm so sorry, honey. The goal was never to deceive you. We just wanted you to have a fresh start, a chance to thrive without the weight of the past on your shoulders. I gave Rose and Mark that photo the day they took you home because, in a way, that was the day you were born into their lives."

I nod as emotion clogs my throat. My parents never intentionally gaslit or mislead me, but they saw my obvious struggles over the years. My mother knew I questioned why I didn't look like them and why she didn't have photos of her pregnancy. The subject would always be changed, my mother never really telling a lie but also never giving me the truth.

"Come on, coffee's ready," Dot says gently as she links her arms through mine and leads us into the kitchen.

A few minutes later, we are seated around Dot's small kitchen table sipping fresh hot coffee. While she didn't have my favorite hazelnut creamer, I suppose the vanilla one she had is getting the job done. I sip the hot liquid and listen intently as she tells me about her late husband, Charles, and how heartbroken she and Annie were when he passed suddenly. Annie was already struggling with depression and manic episodes before his death, but it got much worse after his passing. Then she got pregnant with me, and Annie's mental state declined drastically.

"After you were born, she would be gone for days and return with bloodshot eyes. I could tell she was using; I just wasn't sure what. I found painkillers in her room once, and we had a massive screaming match while you cried in your crib. It wasn't my finest moment, but I felt like I was losing her. That was the day I told her that neither of us could be what you needed." Dot looks mournful as she sips her coffee, her eyes glazing with tears again.

"In the end, I think making her give you up fractured her even further. She never quite recovered, and I saw her less and less over time. I check in on her every week, taking food over to her trailer and leaving it on the porch. Sometimes I'll catch her in a sober moment, and I'll get a glimpse of my daughter, but most days it's just the ghost of her walking around."

My mind spins with the knowledge that my birth mother is an addict and most likely doesn't have the capacity to handle her birth daughter showing up on her doorstep after eighteen years.

But I've come all this way, and I'm not leaving until I look her in the eyes and make sense of the young girl in the polaroid.

"Would you be willing to give me the address to her trailer, Dot?" I ask and receive a nervous glance in return.

"I can, little daisy, but please be careful. Only go over there during the day. There's a lot of sketchy and dangerous people that come and go from that area. I would yank Annie out of there by her hair and drag her home if I thought it would do any good, but it would just push her deeper into their midst." Dot shakes her head and grabs a notepad off the kitchen counter.

"Here," she says as she writes on the paper and hands it to me.

"I don't know what type of state she will be in, Sam. Please don't hold it against her. I think she really tried for so many years, but the darkness won out in the end," Dot explains solemnly.

I can understand that internal battle as I peer down at the healing burn on my wrist. Darkness has a way of finding its way out, one way or another.

I grab the notepad and pen out of her hand and scribble my number on there before passing it back. "Here," I say. "Please call me anytime, I mean it."

"And please, come back and visit anytime. My door is always open for you. For both of you," she says, looking at Ryan and giving him a wink. He bows to her like a court jester, and I roll my eyes at his apparently effective charm.

"I'll be back, I promise," I swear and pull her in for another hug. She walks us back outside, and Ryan and I load into the truck once again. As we reverse out of the drive, I wave to my grandmother and shakily wipe a tear from my cheek.

Now, it's time to find my mother.

Chapter Seventeen

Ryan

Today has been unpredictable, to say the least. This morning, I woke with Sam's body wrapped around mine, her heat enveloping me in a haven of warmth and ecstasy. Then, she shattered every fantasy I've had over the years by pressing her lips to mine. Those fantasies paled in comparison to the reality of Sam's tongue tangling with mine, my teeth biting into her soft lip. The sound of her gasp and moans plays on repeat in my mind. When her hand grazed over my hard dick, I nearly came undone. So, yeah, it's been the best and most unexpected day of my life.

If Sam thinks I'm going to just forget and act like this morning never happened, she's thoroughly mistaken. I saw the way she looked at Dot with an abundance of adoration tinged with fear. She's terrified of letting anyone else in, to get attached just to lose them. Well, I've got news for her; I'm not going anywhere.

Watching Sam meet her grandmother for the first time made every minute of the drive up here worth it. Though I'd drive a hundred hours if it meant having her right next to me. I have no idea what force drove her to kiss me this morning, but to think that she might feel even a fraction of the way that I do is like a dream I never want to wake from.

Sam sits in the passenger seat now as I navigate to the address that her grandmother gave us. The sun is beginning to set overhead, and Sam chews on her nail as we get closer to our destination. Her nerves are palpable as the quaint homes fade in the rearview mirror, and dilapidated buildings give way to a poorly kept side of town.

"You know we can call it a day if you want. Come back tomorrow after you've had time to process all the events of today," I offer, already knowing the answer. There's no way Sam is putting this off for another minute after coming this far.

As expected, she shakes her head and nods to the worn wooden sign coming up on our right that announces our arrival to Willow Pines Trailer Park. The lettering is faded and chipped, and there's a red stain on the bottom of the sign that looks eerily like blood.

"Why wait when we are already here?" She asks with a sureness that doesn't seem to meet her eyes. She wipes her hands on her skirt, her leg bouncing to an anxious rhythm.

I sigh as I pull the truck into the trailer park, driving deeper into it until the GPS stops. An uneasy feeling grows in my gut as the light from the setting sun begins to greet the night. Dot's warning echoes in my mind, and I glance around the park for any commotion but don't see any.

There aren't many trailers in the park, and no signs of toddler bikes or toys on the sparse lawns. Nothing about this space screams family-friendly, unlike many of the trailer parks we passed on the way in.

I kill the truck's engine and reach for my door handle when Sam's hand stops me. I turn to see her looking at me as she nervously bites her lip.

"I can do this one alone," Sam says, though she doesn't sound fully convinced herself. I look back at the trailer in front of us with its broken steps and busted side window that's been duct taped over. I turn back to Sam and scowl at her as if she's grown a second head.

"Absolutely not," I growl and open the door, leaving no room for debate. As much as I respect her desire for privacy with her birth mother, there's no way I'm letting her walk in there without knowing what the situation looks like. If we get in there and everything is fine, I can just step outside and give them the time they need together. But no way in hell is she going in there alone not knowing what we're walking into.

A beat up brown pickup sits parked in front of the trailer letting me know that at least someone is home. My muscles are on high alert as I exit my truck and approach the trailer.

Sam huffs as she slams the passenger door and follows me up the broken steps. Despite her earlier bravado, she freezes when she gets to the front door. She eyes it wearily, and her hand trembles as she raises it into a fist and knocks three times.

Surprisingly, the door opens slightly on its own with an ominous creak. Sam's eyes widen at me, and she lifts her hands in the air innocently.

"I did not do that," She states. I step in front of her and into the doorway before knocking again on the open frame.

"Ms. Mason?" I call out into the dimly lit space. There's a single lamp in the corner lighting the room, and a small, tattered sofa is the only furniture in the living space. The floor is littered with trash and half-finished paintings.

No response comes, and I step further into the home. Sam follows and closes the door behind her, her eyes taking in the messy space.

"Annie?" Sam tries, and the sound of something clattering to the floor comes from down the narrow hall to our right. Sam heads in that direction and stops in front of a cracked bedroom door.

I'm a few steps behind her when she pushes the door open and goes to speak.

"Ann—," her words are cut off abruptly as a tall and lean man charges out of the doorway and grabs her by the throat, throwing her against the wall. Her head bounces off the wood paneling with a sickening thud as the asshole presses into her.

Rage pours into my veins, and I charge at him but stop dead in my tracks when a switchblade suddenly appears against Sam's jaw, just above his grip on her throat. A terrified squeak escapes Sam as her fear-filled eyes find mine.

"Ah-uh," the man says as he trails the tip of the blade along her jawline in an obvious threat. Her face is turning red and small rattles leave her body as she fights for air. My hands fists as my breathing becomes ragged and angry. My eyes frantically search the hallway for anything I can use as a weapon, but there's nothing.

"Let her go," I growl, and the man turns his beady eyes my way. He smiles as he tightens his hold on Sam's throat, lifting her slightly. The tips of her sandals barely graze the floor, and she scratches wildly at his arms.

I'm going to fucking kill this bastard.

"Maybe I will, if you have the money that Annie owes Josiah. Or perhaps," he says as he trails the tip of the blade across Sam's collar bone and around her breast. My vision blurs as her entire body tenses when the man speaks again. "Perhaps, I'll take her with me and see if Josiah can find other ways to collect on Annie's debt."

Without thinking, I let my rage propel me forward. I charge at him, slamming the entirety of my weight into his, sending us flying through the bedroom doorway and crashing to the floor. The knife clatters to the ground somewhere, and I spot Sam sinking to the floor in my periphery, gasping for breath.

I get to my feet just as he does, but he's surprisingly fast. He takes a swing, his fist colliding with my jaw. Pain bursts through my face, and I smile wickedly at him.

"I hope you enjoyed that one," I say, and his eyes widen for a split-second before I lunge and smash my fist into the side of his head, sending him staggering to the floor. He tries to move towards me again, but I sweep his legs out from under him. He crashes to the floor, and I kneel to grasp him in a headlock. The tendons in his neck bulge against my bicep and forearm as his feet kick against the floor.

"How does it feel to be the one fighting for their breath?" I growl into his ear. He thrashes against me and sinks his dirty nails into my forearms. I tighten my hold, wondering how much force it would take to just snap this bastard's neck.

Sam crawls into the doorway holding a hand to her throat and takes in the scene with fear-filled eyes. I never wanted to be a violent person and fuck this man for making me be one.

He never should have touched her.

"Ryan," Sam croaks hoarsely as the man's movements slow. Her pleading gaze pierces my heart, and I lean down to whisper so that only he can hear me.

"You're going to get up and leave, and if you even think about coming near her again, it will be the last thought you ever have," I growl before letting my grip slacken and releasing him. He slumps over and drags in ragged breaths as I move to help Sam off the floor.

I pull her to her feet and take her face in my hands, wiping at the tears sliding down her cheeks.

"Are you okay?" I ask, though I know it's a ridiculous question. She nods anyways, wincing with the movement. Angry red marks paint her neck, and rage barrels through me again. Before I can think about going back over to the bastard and finishing what I started, he stumbles past us and out the front door without looking back.

The desire to go after him and pummel his ass to death is frightening. I resist the urge and pull Sam into the safety of my embrace instead. I wait for a moment, cradling her head against my chest and reveling in the sound of her breathing.

When I'm finally convinced the asshole isn't coming back, I pull away just long enough to grab Sam's hand and guide her down the hallway and into the living room. Before I can move us to the front door, Sam stops me with a tug on my hand. I turn to find her staring up at me with tear-filled eyes.

"Thank you, Ryan," she states with a hoarse and broken voice as she reaches up and gently touches the blossoming bruise on my jaw. I shake my head and press my hand against hers.

"I should have stopped him. He should have never been able to get his hands on you," I say, anger at myself bubbling to the surface. "I'm so sorry, Sam."

"Hey," Sam says softly. "It's no one's fault but his. If you hadn't come in here with me, who knows what would have happened. I'm okay thanks to you, Ryan. No one else, you." Her words douse some of the rage burning in me, and her blue eyes anchor me. I nod against her hand, though the guilt in my chest lingers.

Sam's eyes search mine, and her hand moves from my jaw to the back of my neck. She stands on her tiptoes, and for the second time today, Samatha Grace Miller kisses me. It's slow and sweet, filled with longing and appreciation. I wrap my arms around her waist and press her closer to me. Just as I'm about to deepen the kiss, the front door opens and closes again.

I jerk my head up and instinctively shove Sam behind me. I expect to find the douchebag from earlier coming back for round two, but instead, find a small woman with short blonde hair and familiar blue eyes. She stops abruptly as we come face to face, and before I can speak, Sam's birth mother reaches into her purse and pulls out a handgun. In one swift motion, she flicks off the safety and points the gun directly at my head. My heart stops.

"And who the fuck are you?"

Chapter Eighteen

Sam

"And who the fuck are you?" I hear a feminine voice say right after Ryan abruptly breaks our kiss and shoves himself in front of me. My heartbeat stutters at the sound of what I can only assume is my birth mother's voice.

Ryan lifts one arm up in the air while the other keeps me pressed into his back. I stand on my tiptoes to peer around him, and my breathing stops at the sight of a gun pointed directly at Ryan's face.

"Put the gun down, Ms. Mason," Ryan sates coolly, but the coiled muscles of his back showcase his fear. Annie keeps the gun raised as she spots me behind him.

"How do you know my name, and who's your little friend you're hiding back there? What, did you think you'd break in here and find a score or maybe some cash? Well, hate to break it to you, but you're shit out of luck," Annie says, the arm holding the gun twitching slightly.

Ryan inhales slowly, "No ma'am, that wasn't our intention."

Annie eyes him wearily, gun still trained on his head. I put my hand on his arm and push my way out from behind him.

"Sam—," Ryan begins to protest as Annie's gun moves from him to me.

"It's okay," I say looking to Ryan before turning to meet my birth mother's eyes for the first time. Confusion flickers across her face as she takes in my features. Then, with a soft gasp, she slowly lowers the gun.

"Daisy? You're—you're here?" Annie stares at me with a look of bewilderment. "How?"

"My parents... they died," I say shakily, my throat still hoarse from the recent assault. "They left the truth behind for me to find, and it led me to Dot who sent me here." Sweat gathers in my palms as I take in the woman before me. The years since the polaroid have worn on her, her blonde hair thinner and eyes sunken slightly. She's thin, almost too thin, and there's a consistent tremor in her right hand.

"My mother sent you here?" Annie says as she looks between me and Ryan.

"Yes, and I'm so sorry for the intrusion. The door was open when we got here, and there was an incident. We would have never intentionally invaded your space had we known you weren't here," I explain, still nervously eyeing the gun that hangs from her hand.

Annie's gaze glides from my face to my neck, her eyes widening at what must be a plethora of blossoming bruises if the pain in my throat is any indication. Rage encompasses her face, and she suddenly lifts the gun again, training it on Ryan. I gasp and try to jump in front of him, but he yanks me against his side, pinning me under his arm.

"Don't," Ryan growls at me as I try to break his hold and get in front of him.

"Did you do that to her?" Annie says nodding to my neck while keeping the gun trained on Ryan.

"What?" I ask, confused at the sudden turn of this conversation. Ryan's grip tightens on me, his body going rigid at her words.

"You one of those cowards that needs to beat on a woman to be able to feel like a man, huh?" Annie snarls, and the realization of what she's asking dawns on me. Oh god, no. I instinctively look up at Ryan, and disgust paints his face. My heart shatters at the emotion that rages in his eyes. The blatant accusation that he could be just like the monster that he loathes and fought so hard to escape is ridiculous.

"No—," I go to speak, but Ryan interrupts me.

"I would never hurt her. Or any woman for that matter. I can't say the same for the asshole we caught ransacking the place when we got here. The name Josiah ring a bell?" Ryan asks, anger radiating in his tone. Annie blanches, and fear sweeps over her face.

"Josiah was here?" Her voice quivers, and she lowers the gun and looks at my neck again. "He did that?"

"No," Ryan says. "Not Josiah, just a lackey with a message."

Annie bites at her bottom lip and flips the safety back on the gun before tucking it back into her purse. Ryan's posture relaxes slightly, but he keeps me tucked into his side.

"I'm so sorry, Daisy," Annie says as she steps towards me.

"Um—it's Sam, actually," I state awkwardly, but being called by my birth name just doesn't feel right. It's not the same as the warm nickname Dot used, but more like a foreign identity that I don't recognize.

"Sam, right," Annie says softly, hurt flickering across her face. She shakes her head before walking across the room to sit on the sofa. She motions for me to sit next to her, and I navigate over discarded paintings and trash before sitting. Ryan stays standing off to the side, his arms crossed and eyes weary.

"I'm so sorry, Sam. You should have never been put in harm's way because of my mistakes. It's why I chose to give you away all those years ago; you would have always been in danger with me. I know that's not an excuse because a true mother would never put her child in danger, but I was broken in a way that caused me to break everything around me. I couldn't risk shattering you, too." The heartbreak is Annie's voice is both devastating and healing all at once. She didn't give me away because she didn't want me; she let me go because she loved me too much to risk letting her shadows touch me.

My vision clouds with tears, and a boulder lodges itself in my throat. I'm sitting here next to a woman that I didn't know existed a week ago, yet the way that she speaks makes me feel as if she's been a part of me for years. I recognize the dark fog that I know must plague her, the same darkness that has driven her to pain pills and me to self-harm.

The healing scar on my wrist throbs at the reminder of the abyss that so often calls to me. Annie may have thought that giving me away would keep me innocent and whole, but time still fractured me.

"I understand," I respond, and I do understand. For the first time since finding out about my adoption, I don't feel anger but sympathy for the woman in front of me. Annie shakes her head vigorously.

"No, you don't have to say that. I don't deserve your understanding or forgiveness. You have every right to be angry, Sam."

"You just wanted to protect me. You did the best you could by giving me to two amazing people that did everything they could to keep me safe and loved," I tell her, forcing the words past the lump in my throat. While I'm not angry, I am devastated that my parents couldn't give me the truth while they were still here. For years, I struggled to find comfort in their love because I felt as if I didn't deserve it. I didn't look or act like them, and I constantly felt as if there was a disconnect between us. The icy wall that I presented to ensure they couldn't see all the darkness underneath didn't help our relationship either.

"Your parents," Annie begins. "What happened to them?" A tear slides down her cheek, and she wipes it away with a tremoring hand.

"My mom passed away from cancer five months ago, and my dad had a heart attack last week." The weight of that sentence slams into my chest, and the fog in my brain starts creeping in.

"I'm so sorry," Annie says kindly. "Grief is the heaviest of burdens." Her blue eyes flicker with the memory of her own pain, and I notice then the sweat gathered at her brows and the pallor of her skin.

"Are you okay?" I ask as I nod to her shaking arm. My eyes flick from her to Ryan, and he seems to be tracking the same details as his gaze fixes on her.

"Oh!" Annie exclaims as wipes some of the sweat off her forehead with her trembling hand. "It's just the withdrawals." She smiles sadly, embarrassment creeping into her cheeks.

"Josiah cut me off when I couldn't pay up on my debt, and he'll kill me if he finds me buying from anyone else." Shame paints her features as she wipes another tear away. "I wish I could say I made the decision on my own, but I didn't. And I don't know how much longer I'll last," Annie says honestly.

"But enough about me, I want to know everything there is to know about you," she states enthusiastically. A warm, fuzzy feeling sweeps over me at her words. Knowing that she wants to know me makes my heart clench and increases the size of the rock in my bruised throat.

She isn't turning me away or throwing me out.

She isn't leaving me again.

Before I can find the words to tell her about myself, Ryan glances nervously at the front door. It's dark outside now, and I know this place has him on edge. Every sound coming from the trailer park has his spine straightening and fist clenching. Our earlier encounter with Joshiah's lackey really fucked us both up.

"It's been a really long day for us," I begin, and Annie face drops with disappointment. "We should really call it a night. But if you're feeling up to it, maybe we could go for lunch somewhere tomorrow and take some time to talk?" The last few words come out shaky as my nerves begin to get the better of me. Annie face lights up, disappointment completely replaced by eagerness.

"I would love that. I'll give you my number and you can tell me when and where, and I'll be there, Sam. I promise," She finishes with a gentle touch of her hand on my knee. I place my hand over hers and grab my phone from my skirt pocket.

After I get her number entered, we stand and begin towards the door.

"Are you going to be okay here?" I ask, remembering the very recent intruder that was in her home. Annie just smiles and nods towards her purse.

"I got good aim. I'll be just fine," she says confidently.

"Okay," I say awkwardly, not sure if I should offer to hug her before leaving or not. I opt for a small wave which she returns, and then I grab Ryan's hand and head to the truck.

"It was an honor to meet you, Sam," Annie calls from the doorway, and I stop midway into the truck.

"Goodnight, Annie," I say with another wave before climbing into the passenger side and closing the door. I watch as she enters her home again and think about how drastically different my life would have been if she had raised me here. The idea makes me crave the warmth and comfort of my childhood home with my mom and dad surrounding me.

Just a week ago, I was vilifying my parents for showing another child love for so many years. Now, I realize just how lucky both

Ryan and I were to be loved by them.

Perspective is a fickle thing, and as I look over at Ryan driving us out of the trailer park and to a nearby motel, I realize that there are quite a few things I'm starting to see in a new light.

Chapter Nineteen

Sam

When we get to the motel, I grab us a room while Ryan gets our bags. The clerk eyes me wearily as he takes in the fresh bruising on my neck, but he doesn't say anything. He just hands me the keycard and points me on my way.

I meet Ryan back at the entrance and help take our few bags to room 112. When I unlock the room and step inside, Ryan lets out a small laugh.

"Let me guess, this was the last room they had?" He asks as he takes in the single queen size bed. I look between him and the bed and shrug my shoulders casually. Heat rushes to my cheeks, and I try to play it off.

"No, I just didn't specify how many beds we needed. Would you prefer I go back down there and get a room with two beds?" I ask, raising my eyebrows at him.

"Not a chance," Ryan states, a mischievous look creeping into his eyes.

I roll my eyes and fight a smile as I move to one side of the bed and set my bag on it. I grab a change of clothes and walk past Ryan to the bathroom. Once inside, I look into the mirror and gasp. My neck is marred with shades of black and purple, and the memory of that creep's hand around my throat and his body against mine makes my stomach turn in a dizzying wave of nausea.

I brace my hands against the counter and take steadying breaths to keep myself from vomiting. I knew that Annie probably wouldn't be in the healthiest of places, but she's clearly in a very bad spot with some seriously violent people. What happens to her if she can't pay her debt to this Josiah guy?

I try to shake the thoughts from my mind as I wash my face, brush my teeth, and change into a baggy tee and pajama shorts. I use the restroom and come back out to find Ryan waiting outside the door with his change of clothes in hand. He looks at me nervously as if he were afraid I'd have a breakdown in the bathroom.

"It wouldn't be the first time," I think as I just smile at him and motion for him to take his turn in the bathroom.

"It's all yours," I say casually, and he just nods before going inside. There's an odd tension between us right now that I can't quite pinpoint the cause of. It has been an unorthodox few days, and we did have a rather traumatic evening. Maybe we both just need some food and some sleep. I realize then that we haven't eaten all day, so I order a pizza and soda delivery on my phone and scroll the tv options for a movie. I find one and snicker as I pause the screen and wait on Ryan.

A few minutes later, he emerges from the bathroom in grey sweats and a white t-shirt. His brown hair is lightly mussed, and the purple and blue painting his left jaw brings out the grey in his stormy blue eyes. My heart clenches at the memory of him tackling Josiah's lackey to the ground, the knife falling away from my chest, and Ryan nearly strangling the life out of him.

Who knows what would have happened if he hadn't gone inside

with me.

I must be staring, because Ryan lifts a hand to his jaw and asks, "Is it that bad?"

"You should see the other guy," I joke lightheartedly. It seems to work as I'm granted the appearance of one of Ryan's illuminous smiles.

"I hope we never have the displeasure of seeing that fucker again," Ryan says, his smile dropping. He walks toward me and stops a breath away. I tilt my head up to look at him, and he reaches out to lightly caress the curve of my bruised neck. A pained look flashes over his face, and he pulls his hand away from my neck, curling it into a fist by his side. He seems to be restraining himself, but from what, I don't know.

"What?" I ask, sensing that earlier tension rising between us again.

"I just—have this all-consuming need to touch you, to map out and feel every part of your body to make sure you're really okay." His words ignite a heat inside of me that rushes to my core as his eyes trail up and down my body. "But you're not mine to touch, Samantha."

My breath catches as I take in the muscles flexing in his arms, fighting to restrain himself.

I take that last step, closing the distance between us and take his hand in mine. Then I guide his hand to rest on the curve of my ass as I lean up on my tiptoes and wrap my arms around his neck.

"Touch me, Ryan," I whisper, and the wall of restraint shatters around us. Ryan grabs my ass in both his hands and lifts me into the air, wrapping my legs around his waist. Then, his lips are on mine in a crash of ecstasy. I moan into his mouth and thread my fingers through his hair, giving it a rough tug. His teeth clamp around my bottom lip in response, and my core pulses with excitement.

Ryan walks us forward, our tongues still creating a painting of euphoria until he lays me down on the bed and breaks the kiss to kneel over me.

"Tell me you want this, Samantha, because once I've tasted you, I won't be able to go back to the way things were. I'll never get enough," Ryan says, his gaze darkening as he takes in my body below him.

I lean up and grip the bottom of his shirt, tugging it over his head. It falls to the floor as I run my fingers along the ridges of his abs.

"I want you, Ryan," I say, my voice sounding heavy with need. That's all it takes for him to crash back into me, his mouth colliding with mine as we fall back against the pillows.

Ryan's hand slides under my shirt as our tongues tangle with each other's, and he grabs my breast with a rough squeeze. Pleasure shoots through me when he takes my nipple between his fingers and lightly pinches. I break the kiss to gasp in ecstasy, and he takes the cue to tweak my nipple harder. I moan again, the sound foreign to my ears. Pain has always anchored me, but it's never given me pleasure—not like this.

Ryan releases my breast and bends his head down to gently kiss my neck. The hand under my shirt slides down to the waistband of my shorts and pushes past the fabric. His fingers instantly find my clit and begin torturously slow circles that send me careening up a mountain of pleasure. He lifts his head to look into my eyes, his eyes burning with a feverish passion.

His fingers move from my clit to glide through my folds, and I gasp loudly, my body vibrating with the need for more.

"Mmm, I never thought I'd see the day where your pussy would weep for me, Samantha," Ryan says with a satisfied hum. Before I can even process his words, he slams two fingers inside of me while his thumb meets my clit again.

I cry out in pleasure, my back arching off the bed as Ryan thrusts his fingers in and out while circling my clit in a destructive rhythm. Pressure builds in my core and pushes me higher up that mountain of pleasure.

My mouth falls open in a silent gasp, and Ryan's gaze darkens as he watches my body writhe underneath his touch. He adds another finger, hitting a spot in me that has stars dancing in my vision.

"That's it, baby, come for me," Ryan says as he circles my clit one more time. His words send me tumbling off that mountain in an avalanche of ecstasy as an orgasm rips through my body. I cry out, hands fisting in the pillows under me as my eyes roll with the ripples of pleasure coursing through me.

I watch with a hooded gaze as Ryan pulls his hand out of my shorts and presses closer into me, his bulging cock rubbing against me through his sweats. I reach for the waistband of his pants but freeze when a knock sounds at the door.

Ryan's posture goes rigid above me as he looks at me in confusion. My expression mimics his own until realization dawns on me.

"The pizza!" I say, slapping my hand against my forehead. "I ordered dinner," I say sheepishly, moving up some in the bed to put space between us.

"But I'd much rather eat you," Ryan states coolly, and my jaw drops as I watch him bring his fingers to his mouth and consume the remnants of my orgasm with a moan. Heat flares across my cheeks, and he grins, dropping his hand back down before standing. I'm still frozen in place when Ryan adjusts his pants and goes to answer the door.

He returns a moment later with the pizza and drinks. He winks at me as he sets the pizza on the bed, and I shakily scoot over to make room for him. My body is still vibrating from the orgasm, and I'm not entirely sure I'll ever recover.

Ryan hands me a piece of pizza on a napkin and then grabs his own.

"Don't worry, I'll save room for dessert," he says with a grin, and the heat in my cheeks burns at a new degree.

"Oh my god, you're incorrigible," I say as I grab the remote and turn on the paused movie to try and distract myself from the feel of him next to me. Reese Witherspoon fills the screen in a sexy bunny costume, and I grin.

"Legally Blonde, really?" Ryan asks, and I laugh.

"It's a classic," I say, feeding his words back to him from the night before.

"Can't argue with you on that," Ryan states as he takes a bite of his pizza. I do the same as we let the sounds of Reese Witherspoon's comedic whips diminish the tension around us.

Chapter Twenty

Ryan

I've always known that Sam owned a piece of me that no one else could touch. Watching her over the years was such a comforting distraction from my own personal turmoil. I would look forward to family dinners at Mark and Rose's table where I could sit across from Sam and try to dissect her every emotion. How could a girl that seemingly had everything I craved be so sad and lonely?

I never felt spiteful about it though, just intrigued. I would count down the moments until I could see her again, just to pester her and see how much it would take to make her squirm. My presence would bring an irritated anger to her eyes, and I would revel in it because it was so much better to see than the sad dejected look she often wore.

Last night, however, the fire in her eyes wasn't anger, but pleasure fueled by my touch. Feeling her writhe beneath me and come undone on my fingers absolutely solidified just how much she owns me.

After getting out of Annie's trailer, all I wanted to do was grab

Sam and slam my lips into hers, to feel the warmth and life in every curve of her body and know that she was alive and safe. But then, I had to remind myself that she isn't mine to touch. My restraint was being tested though when she exited the bathroom dressed in those tiny pajama shorts and baggy shirt, wrapped in the smell of coconut body spray.

Then, she said those words, and I came undone. After one taste, I am unequivocally consumed by Samantha Grace Miller.

After pizza last night, I could see the day beginning to wear on her as she yawned and rubbed at her eyes. As much as I would have loved to go for another round of seeing how quickly I could make her cum, it just wasn't the right time. While I taunted her about dessert, I knew it would have to wait until another day.

We drifted off to sleep facing each other, and Sam, once again, slept soundly through the night.

"Ugh!" Sam exclaims in frustration from the bathroom. I snap back to the present and move into the open door to see what the hold up is. We are supposed to be meeting Annie in thirty minutes at a Mexican place not too far from here. Sam's already dressed in high-rise jean shorts that hug her perfectly round ass and a black Vincent Van Gogh t-shirt. Her blonde waves fall effortlessly down her back, and she wears a small amount of makeup that accentuates her sharp facial features. She's fucking breathtaking.

The hold up, however, is the makeup she is currently trying to apply to her neck to cover the fresh bruising. She uses a little egg-shaped sponge to blot concealer onto the markings. It helps some, but the worst of the bruising still peeks out from the layers of makeup.

"It's okay, Sam. You look beautiful," I tell her as I approach her from behind and place a gentle kiss to the side of her neck. Her eyes meet mine in the mirror, and she smiles softly. Sam's smile isn't something I'm used to seeing it, and it's quickly becoming my favorite sight in the world.

"Thank you, I'm just freaking out a little bit," she says. "I'm not sure what to expect from today, and I feel like we got off to an awkward start with Annie yesterday."

"Oh, you mean when she pointed a gun at our faces. Nah, that wasn't awkward at all," I joke with a grin. It eases some of Sam's tension as she laughs, too.

"Also, you don't look too bad yourself," Sam states as she turns and lets her eyes roam up and down my body. I'm wearing dark jeans and a grey shirt that hugs my biceps perfectly. I'm not ashamed to admit that I chose it purely because I've seen Sam stealing glances at the muscles of my arms when she thinks I'm not looking.

I grin again and turn to step out of the bathroom. "We should get going if we want to get there on time," I tell Sam, holding my hand out to her. She nods, packing her makeup back up and giving herself a once over in the mirror.

"Okay, let's go," she says, letting out a deep breath. She grabs my hand, and we walk out of the motel to load into the truck. I turn on a pop playlist as I drive, and Sam picks at her nails while bouncing her leg in the passenger seat. I reach my hand over and rest it on her bouncing thigh, and it stills underneath my touch. I can feel the nervous energy radiating through her skin.

"Hey, it's going to be okay. You owe her nothing, and there's no expectations of you here," I say calmly. Sam looks at me with wide eyes and lets out another deep sigh.

"I just don't want to mess up. I don't want to give up too much of myself to Annie that it somehow dishonors the memory of my parents, but I also don't want to say too much about them that it upsets Annie and compromises her recovery. It feels like an eggshell situation, and I don't want anyone to get hurt," Sam explains with a sad smile. I give her leg a comforting squeeze, and her hand lands on top of mine to thread through my fingers.

"You aren't in any way responsible for Annie or her recovery. She is an adult who makes her own decisions. As for your parents, they would never hold your curiosity and desire to connect with your birth mother against you. That wasn't the type of people they were. If anything, I think they would be proud of how far you've come in your willingness to put your emotions out there rather than keeping them bottled up, unwilling to act on what you want or feel. They only ever wanted you to be happy, Samantha," I say, and her hand squeezes around mine at my words.

I look over to see tears in Sam's eyes as she smiles at me.

"Thank you," she whispers. I swallow the lump in my throat as I navigate us into the restaurant parking lot. I can only imagine the complexity of emotions Sam must be feeling right now. To go from losing both of your parents to discovering you were adopted and finding your birth mother? It's a lot for anyone, but a part of me wishes I could understand it, wishes that my parents weren't really my parents, and I had some long-lost parents out there that weren't abusive alcoholics. Unfortunately, my chances of having that unconditional parental love died with Mark and Rose.

I park the truck and turn off the ignition as I scan the area for any sign of Annie. If she bails on Sam and sends her careening back into the darkness, I might just find myself back at the trailer park with a gun in my face.

Luckily, I spy her short blonde hair and slender frame standing outside the restaurant entrance. She looks around nervously, biting on her bottom lip.

I look next to me to find Sam wearing the same expression as she spots Annie. She chews anxiously on her lip as well, and I reach out and grab her chin between my fingers, turning her toward me.

"Relax, you've got this," I say as I use my thumb to glide over her bottom lip until she releases it from her teeth.

"If you get too deep in your head and need to distract your thoughts, just think of this moment," I say, and I lean forward and capture her mouth with my own. She gasps, and I swallow the sound as I devour the taste of her. I swirl my tongue around hers, and she moans softly.

Reluctantly, I pull back and take in her flushed face and pink lips. Her blue eyes are alight with desire, and I grin as I move to exit the truck.

"And just think of all the things I can do with my tongue later," I say with a wink before opening the door and getting out. I look back through the windshield to see Sam clamoring to get out, flustered but clearly distracted from her earlier nerves.

She slams her door and walks past me towards the entrance, her cheeks somehow redder than they had been before.

"You're an ass," she grumbles as she passes, and I let out a laugh as I follow her. Oh, this day is going to be interesting.

Chapter Twenty-One

Sam

Annie sits across from me at lunch looking worse than she did last night. Dark circles shadow her eyes, her skin is painted with a sheen of sweat, and the tremors are more prominent today. It's obvious that Josiah cutting her off is taking its toll on her body.

"Are you okay?" I ask her as the waitress drops chips and salsa off to our table. The waitress eyes Annie wearily as if afraid she might drop dead at any second. Honestly, I can't blame her. My birth mother looks a breath away from collapsing.

"Oh, I'm fine," Annie says, waving off my concern. She reaches for a chip with a trembling hand and takes a bite of it, seemingly forcing herself to chew and swallow it. I don't call her out on the obvious lie, though.

"This is Ryan, by the way," I say, gesturing to Ryan who sits in a relaxed posture beside me. His arm is casually thrown over the back of my chair, and his fingers occasionally brush against my shoulder. His touch, however light, sends shivers through me as my mind replays the events of last night.

I try to shake the memory from my thoughts and focus on Annie.

"We didn't really get to do formal introductions yesterday, but he's my neighbor," I state, uncertainty lacing the last word. Calling him my neighbor feels odd suddenly, as if the term is too impersonal. But what else can I refer to him as? He's not my boyfriend, and I don't think 'the guy that made me see stars last night' is an appropriate introduction in any scenario. Friend, perhaps?

Ryan tilts his head at me with a lopsided grin.

"Yeah, we're real neighborly," he says and licks his lips as if tasting the memory of the kiss we shared earlier. Heat floods my body at the reminder, and I kick his leg under the table. A grunt leaves his mouth and quickly turns into a chuckle. Annie eyes us with an amused look, a small smile playing on her lips.

"Well, Ryan, I apologize for the way I greeted you yesterday. Needless to say, I've been on edge. It's been a chaotic few days, and I'm sorry that both of you got caught up in it," Annie says, empathy dripping from her words.

"We were in your home without your permission. I think your reaction was quite reasonable," Ryan states seriously. Annie just nods, and I wonder for the first time today if she has the gun in her purse still. Is it safe for her to be carrying around a weapon while going through withdrawals? There's no way she has a license for it, right? It dawns on me then just how little I know about the woman sitting in front of me.

"When is your birthday?" I ask abruptly. Annie looks at me in surprise before answering.

"October 20th. And yours is February 15th," she says with a reminiscent smile that makes my heart squeeze.

"I could never forget that date. I may not have been able to be the parent that you needed, but the day that you were born was the greatest day of my life," Annie tells me, tears brimming in her blue eyes.

"I had never felt such pain as I did when giving birth to you. But then you were laid in my arms, and none of the pain mattered. You were the most beautiful little flower I'd ever seen." A few tears fall down her cheeks, and I feel my eyes stinging with moisture as well.

"Cradling you in my arms made me want to paint the world with the most radiant colors just so everyone else could see just a glimpse of the brightness that you brought to my soul." Her words cause my throat to tighten. Ryan reaches under the table to rest his hand on my thigh. He gives it a gentle squeeze as Annie continues to speak.

"I can't imagine what it felt like for you to find out about the adoption, but I need you to know that you weren't adopted because I didn't want you. I had to give you up because I wanted you to live and to be loved safely. I could never have given you the life that Mark and Rose did. When I met them, I could see that same desire to love and protect you in their eyes. I knew then that they were meant to be your home," Annie says with a sad smile.

"I'm so sorry that I couldn't be that home for you," she states softly. A tear escapes my eye, and I wipe it away and sniffle.

"It's okay," I whisper, and I'm surprised to realize that I mean it. After seeing Annie's life now, I know that having her as my mother would have meant a life of survival and instability. While I dealt with my own demons over the last few years, my parents never once made me feel unsafe. Even during the worst of my spirals, they still tried to make me feel as loved and protected as they could.

The waitress comes by then to collect our orders. If she hears the shakiness in our voices and sees the tear tracks on our faces, she doesn't say anything. When she leaves, I turn back to Annie and take a steadying breath.

"What about my father?" I ask the question that's been bouncing in my mind since the day I found out about the adoption. A grimace crosses Annie's face, and I brace myself for whatever she's about to say.

"In high school, I dated a guy off and on for a while. He was the kindest and smartest person, but my instability caused serious issues in our relationship. He didn't have the best home life, and he didn't really agree with the people I chose to hang around. I always knew he was destined for better things, and when he got a scholarship out of state, I knew that was it for us. He wanted me to go with him, but I refused. I knew I would just hold him back," she says sadly.

"When I found out I was pregnant, he was getting ready to leave and start a fresh chapter. I couldn't shatter that new life, so instead I broke his heart. I said some very cruel things that guaranteed he would never look back, and then he left. He never even knew I was pregnant. He doesn't know you exist, Sam. I'm so sorry." Her voice cracks as fresh tears fall from her eyes. Her words bounce around my brain as emotion clogs my throat.

"He never knew about me?" I ask dumbfounded. He was never even given the chance to love me.

"I'm so sorry, Sam," Annie says with a soft sob. Before I can gather my thoughts to respond, a tall, muscular man with sharp features, dark hair, and brown eyes falls into the chair next to Annie. She instantly stiffens as he drapes his arm around her shoulder and pulls her into him.

"Oh, Annie bear, a little birdie told me you were here," the man says in a menacingly deep voice that sends shivers of fear down my spine.

"J—Josiah," Annie breathes, and Ryan and I go rigid in our seats.

Josiah turns to look at us with a bright smile. His features are handsome and intimidating, and he looks to be a few years younger than Annie. He appears suave in his dark jeans, black button down, and boots. He isn't anything like the haggard looking guy that attacked us at Annie's house.

"Well, hello," Josiah purrs as he looks at me. His eyes scan my face with scrutiny before he lets out a small chuckle. "Oh, Annie. You didn't tell me you had a daughter. And a beautiful one at that. Though, I would expect nothing less from you," Josiah says, turning his gaze to Annie and reaching out to tuck a hair behind her ear. She trembles under his touch, and the intimacy of the movement makes me think there's more to their relationship than just dealer and user.

Ryan's hand is cutting off the circulation in my leg now as we both take in the situation in front of us. The waitress comes by then with our plates of food and sets them out. She glances around us with uncertainty before asking Josiah if he would like to order anything. Without even looking at her, he just waves his hand in the air dismissively. She scoffs and walks off, decidedly ignoring the tension at the table.

"She isn't my daughter. She's just one of those do-gooders who wanted to buy the local nutcase some lunch. I was just telling her I don't need charity," Annie says harshly. She aggressively swipes at the wetness on her cheeks as if trying to erase any proof of our intimate conversation. Though I know she's just trying to protect me, her words slice through my heart.

"Yeah, we were just leaving," Ryan states in a deep tone. His eyes are dark and his jaw ticks as he eyes Josiah.

Josiah just grins and shakes his head. "No need to rush out on a perfectly good meal. I'll be on my way," he says as he stands, releasing his hold on Annie.

"I just came to give my sweet Annie here a message," Josiah states, and he leans down into Annie's space. "I expect your debt to be paid in full within the next 24 hours, or I'll have to start making some rounds. Perhaps I'll stop in to see that sweet mother of yours. What was her name, again? Dot?" Annie pales at his words, and rage fills my veins.

"I wouldn't recommend that," Ryan growls, and Josiah turns to look at him with a condescending gaze.

"I assume you're the little shit that got the one-up on Ronnie, hmm? Funny that a simple good Samaritan and her boytoy would just be walking into the home of an addict while she isn't there, but what do I know," Josiah states, giving me a knowing look. Annie's earlier words aren't fooling him, and his eyes look as if they are actively painting a target on my forehead.

"Just remember, Annie, I don't like to be kept waiting," Josiah says, looking between me and Annie once more before turning and walking out of the restaurant. A collective breath of relief shudders through the air around us.

"What the fuck was that?" I ask Annie in a shaky tone.

"That," Annie begins, smoothing her hair nervously with shaking hands. "Was the reaper."

Chapter Twenty-Two

Sam

"I'm sorry, 'the reaper'?" I ask Annie because, surely, I heard wrong. What small town drug dealer goes by a pretentious nickname like 'the reaper'?

"I don't know where or when it started, but that's what the people in his crew call him. It's a reminder of the death that he leaves in his wake. He doesn't just deal drugs, Sam. He's a very dangerous person who will stop at nothing to avenge himself if he feels even a little slighted. I should have never brought you into his orbit," Annie says, shaking her head vigorously.

"What are you going to do then? Do you have the money you owe him?" I question, though I can already guess the answer. Annie shakes her head again, and my heart sinks.

"No, but I'll figure it out. Just please stay far away from him. This doesn't concern you," Annie says matter-of-factly. "I will handle it later, but right now, I refuse to let him ruin this lunch."

She clears her throat, clearly dropping the subject. "Now, tell me about yourself, Sam."

So, for the next thirty minutes, I tell Annie all about my

childhood. I tell her about my passion for drawing but how I've never dabbled in painting. She listens intently as I describe how warm and kind my mother, Rose, was and how devastating it was to watch cancer slowly take her away from us. I even tell her about that awful fight I had with my dad right before he died, how those were the last words I ever spoke to him.

Silent tears slide down her cheeks as I tell her about finding him on the floor after my graduation. Ryan's hand is a steadying anchor on my leg, and it feels like a catharsis of some sort to get it all out.

I don't tell her about the darkness, though, that I've battled with over the recent years. I don't divulge the loneliness that would keep me awake at night or how I never felt like I fit perfectly with Mark and Rose despite their best efforts. It seems unfair to tell her those things, and I'm afraid she would fault herself for those feelings and the subsequent self-harm that resulted from them.

So, I keep those little parts of myself locked away while I let the rest out for her to see. Annie asks me about my favorite color, the food I like most, what music I listen to, and if I have any pets. I answer each question with a little more information than necessary, and Ryan chimes in with anecdotes about how I was as a child.

We finish our food, somehow not letting Josiah's earlier appearance ruin the whole date. When the bill arrives, Annie looks embarrassed as I reach over and collect it. I don't draw attention to it, just slide my card into the bifold and hand it back to the waitress.

When we walk out of the restaurant and into the parking lot, Annie stops me with a hand on my wrist.

"Thank you," she says softly, and I know she means for more than just lunch. I nod and swallow the lump in my throat, and then I surprise myself by throwing my arms around her. She lets out a startled gasp before bringing her arms around my back to hug me.

"Thank you for giving me the answers I needed," I say genuinely. We break the hug, and Annie nods.

"Will I see you again? There's still so much I need to learn about you, little daisy," Annie states, and her voices breaks on the last part.

"Of course, I'll call you, okay?" I tell her, and we hug one last time. Annie looks at me like she's committing my face to memory before she turns to look at Ryan.

"And you," she begins, pointing a finger at him. Ryan quirks an eyebrow, clearly unsure of what she's going to say. "Take care of her, please."

Ryan looks my way and smiles. "Until the day my heart stops beating," he says, and Annie grins in return. Oh, God, he's so corny.

"Can we give you a ride?" I ask as Annie turns to walk away. She stops and looks our way before shaking her head.

"No, the walk will do me some good. I'll text you when I make it home, okay?" She says, and I nod. Then, she turns and walks away. Something uncomfortable knots itself in my stomach as I watch her retreating form. How in the hell is she going to get Josiah off her back before his timeclock is up? I stand there worrying at my bottom lip until Ryan's hands land on my shoulders and his lips glide against my ear.

"Come on, let's get you back," he says, and I shiver at the deep timbre of his voice.

"Do you think she'll be okay?" I ask as I turn to look up into his stormy eyes. His hands come up to cup my face as he answers.

"Judging by the daughter that she created, I can guarantee you that she is a strong-willed fighter of a woman. She's resilient," Ryan says, and the way he looks at me sends heat coursing through my veins.

I've always found Ryan attractive, but the last few days I've begun to find my pulse quickening at the slightest glimpse of him. My core pulses at the sight of his back muscles flexing when he bends over or the flash of the small dimple in his left cheek when he smiles. I'm becoming completely consumed by everything he says or does. He's started something in me that I can't control, and the need to level the playing field is overwhelming.

An idea begins to form in my mind, and I bite my lip to hide my smile.

"You're right," I say as I break away from Ryan and head to the truck. He follows and climbs in, cranking it and turning on his pop playlist. My heart pounds as a nervous vibration runs through my body. Ryan navigates us through the busier streets and onto the backroad that I know we will be on for a few minutes. The cloudiness overhead dims the truck cabin, and I take a deep steadying breath. I can do this—I want to do this. My body heats with anticipation, and I feel as if I'm on the verge of combusting.

I check the road for any cars nearby and see none. With one last deep breath, I unbuckle my seatbelt and lean across the gear shift. Ryan looks at me in surprise, a slightly concerned look passing over his face.

"What are you doing?" He asks, and I answer by reaching down and unbuttoning his pants. His breath catches, and my hands shake as my eyes look up to meet his heated gaze.

"Leveling the playing field," I say with a smirk as I pull out his already half-hard cock. A moan leaves his lips, sending shivers of victory through me. There's something electrifying about knowing that I can make him feel as frazzled as I felt last night.

I give him a couple of long, hard strokes, bringing his smooth cock to its full glorious height.

"S—Sam," he stutters, and I lean down to lick the head. He hisses another moan, and I slide the tip into my mouth.

"Sam, your throat," Ryan says gruffly, concern and desire warring with each other. I pull my head back to look up at him briefly. Desire burns in his eyes as he flicks his gaze from the road to me.

"If my throat is going to hurt, I want it to be because I took you so deep that I'll feel you for days." My heady voice is unrecognizable as I speak. "Just try not to wreck us, okay?" I say, and without another word, I take him in my mouth again.

His thick penis pulses against my tongue, precum coating my tastebuds. My mouth salivates, and I take him deeper and deeper until he's hitting the back of my throat. I swirl my tongue at the base and then pull back up to the head before going all the way back down again.

Ryan hisses in pleasure, one hand coming down to fist in my hair. His grip sends heat flooding to my core, and I moan around his cock.

"Jesus, Sam," his voice sounds raspy and unsteady. I smile around him as I come up and down again and again. Making him feel out of control after years of him trying to get under my skin feels glorious. My clit throbs as I work his cock with my mouth. His legs twitch underneath me, and his grip tightens in my hair. I quicken my pace and glide up and down the length of him until he groans my name again. Then, warm, salty liquid shoots to the back of my throat, and I swallow every last drop.

I release him from my mouth and lean back into the passenger seat with a victorious grin. Ryan wipes a hand down his face before tucking himself back into his pants.

"You're going to pay for that," Ryan states while pointing a finger at me as if knowing that I was trying to one-up him. Tingles shoot through me at his words, and my grin widens.

"Can't wait," I say tauntingly as Ryan navigates us off the backroad and into the motel parking lot.

"Good," he says as he slides the truck into park. "Because I'm about to devour you, Samantha."

Chapter Twenty-Three

Ryan

Anticipation buzzes in my veins as I lead us into the motel room. Sam follows a few steps behind, her confident stride turning more nervous with each step. As much as I pride myself on my ability to always get a rise out of Sam, it was she who completely unraveled me back in the truck. When she suddenly unbuckled her belt and leaned across the center, my brain short-circuited.

Then, she was unbuttoning my pants and taking my length into her hand, guiding me into her mouth. When her plump lips wrapped around my cock and her silken tongue slid against my skin, it took everything in me not to finish right then. I fisted my hand in her hair, trying to grasp a sliver of control, but then she moaned around my cock, and I was done for.

She swallowed every drop of cum and then pulled back to give me a triumphant grin. She thinks she's won in this game of orgasmic chess, but I'm about to make her scream my name in the ultimate checkmate.

We enter the room, and Sam nervously takes her shoes off as I close the door and bolt it. The click of the lock echoes through the space, and my muscles vibrate with need. I turn around to find Sam rummaging through her bag, seemingly trying to distract herself and ignore the potent energy around us.

"Did you enjoy that?" I ask Sam as I take a step in her direction. She quits rummaging in her bag and stands, taking a step back and then another. I match her steps, closing the gap between us as she backs herself into the wall.

"What do you mean?" Sam asks, her voice a husky whisper as her eyes shimmer with anticipation. I take one last step until my chest is pressed against hers and my form towers over her, boxing her in.

"Unraveling me," I say as I reach down and grab both her wrists in my hands and raise them up to press into the wall above her head. Her chest heaves against mine, and she clenches her thighs together. Red creeps across her cheeks, and her pupils dilate with arousal.

"Well, it's my turn now," I say, pressing my hips into hers. "And when I'm done, you will be so irrevocably mine, there will be no distinguishing where I end and you begin," I finish, and I slam my mouth against hers. Sam moans and opens for me, her tongue flicking out to meet my own. I press her wrists harder against the wall as she stands on her tiptoes, her body pliant beneath me.

Sam hikes a leg around my waist, pushing her hips further into me. I break our kiss and release Sam's wrists to rip her shirt off and then my own. Sam looks divine as she eyes me with a heated look, her lips puffy and her round tits pushed up perfectly in a teal bra.

I kick off my shoes and pants, leaving myself clad in my boxers. Sam's gaze roams up and down my body appreciatively, and without breaking eye contact, she reaches behind her back and unclasps her bra. Her perky breasts bounce free, and my dick hardens further.

"Shorts, too," I command, and she stares at me in a silent challenge as she unbuttons her shorts and slides them down her body. She kicks them away, leaving her wearing just a teal lace thong that accentuates the curve of her hips. The scars on her inner thighs are prominent against her otherwise smooth skin.

"Beautiful," I whisper as I close the distance between us again. I slide down onto my knees in front of her, and a look of astonishment passes over Sam's face.

"What are you doing?" She asks in a shaky voice.

"Worshipping you," I tell her as I grab her right leg and place it over my shoulder. A gasp leaves her lips as I lean down and press delicate kisses to each of the scars on her thighs. Then, I pull her thong to the side with one hand and use the other to glide a single finger through the glistening folds of her pussy. Her body trembles at the small touch, and I grin up at her teasingly.

"I should have known all that hatred you had for me was just misdirected desire, Samantha, because you are dripping wet," I say as I plunge my finger inside of her. Sam gasps and bucks her hips, her hand coming down to tangle into my hair. She gives it a tug, drawing my head back to look up at her.

"I thought you were going to devour me," she purrs, her core clenching around my finger at her own words. My dick twitches, and I swear I want to spend the rest of my life on my knees for her.

"Careful what you ask for," I say, and I lean forward to lick along her folds. She trembles and moans, and I know I'll be dreaming of that sound for the rest of my life. The taste of her wetness is intoxicating, and I moan against her. Then, I'm feasting on her as I thrust my tongue inside of her pussy. My finger moves in tandem with my tongue, and Sam's grip on my hair tightens as she pushes her hips into my face. I add another finger and move my tongue up to circle her clit. The second I hit the bundle of nerves, Sam lets out a gasp and grips my hair painfully. I lightly bite her clit in return, and she cries out in pleasure.

"Oh, God, Ryan," Sam breathes. "Don't stop." I take that as my cue to add a third finger in and suck her clit between my teeth, giving it a harder tug this time before caressing it with languid strokes of my tongue. On the third bite, Sam convulses around my fingers and cries out. She grips my hair tightly as her body shudders, painting my fingers and chin with her cum.

I hum against her and kiss her clit before pulling my fingers out and easing her leg back down to the floor. When I stand and take in her appearance, my cock grows impossibly harder. Her cheeks are flushed, and her eyes are glazed with the afterglow of pleasure. Her thong sits askew on her hips, and I walk forward to pull it down and out from around her ankles. I toss it across the room and then step out of my boxers.

Sam's mouth drops open, and my cock pulses at the memory of being swallowed down her throat.

"Get on the bed before I fuck you right against this wall," I growl. Sam shivers, her nipples hardening at my words. She stumbles the few steps to the bed and climbs on, laying back to prop herself up on her elbows. Her heated eyes track my movements as I reach down into my pants pocket on the floor, grab my wallet, and remove the square foil package.

I put the foil between my teeth and rip it open. Keeping my eyes on Sam's, I roll the condom over my hard cock and climb onto the bed. Sam's legs instinctively drop open, her center still glistening from her earlier orgasm. She looks fucking heavenly. I glide my cock against her entrance and lean down to trail kisses down her neck.

"Fuck me already, Ryan," Sam huffs in frustration as she drags her nails down my back. I laugh against her throat and bring a hand up to cup her breast. She moans as I tweak her nipple and tease her entrance with my cock.

"Ryan—," she pants, and I can't hold back anymore. I twist her nipple and bite her neck as I thrust deep into her. Sam cries out, and I lift my head to look into her eyes as I find my rhythm inside of her. Her heat wraps around me, and her walls squeeze my cock as if welcoming me home. Sam moans, her eyes rolling and eyelids drooping closed in an overload of pleasure. I cup her jaw and pull her face close to mine, her eyes fluttering back open as I thrust deeper.

"Eyes on me when I'm making love to you, Samantha," I state, and her eyes widen as she trembles beneath me.

"Don't," Sam whispers, and my thrusts slow as I try to comprehend what she's saying.

"Don't what?" I ask, my movements stalling when a single tear slides down her cheek.

"You can't fall in love with me," she says softly, but her body betrays her words as her pussy squeezes my cock at the thought of me loving her. I resume my thrusts and wipe away her single tear. Her lips part in a silent gasp as I hit the sensitive wall inside of her repeatedly. I move my hand down to roll my thumb over her clit, and her body tightens, her hands coming up to grip my shoulders.

"Oh, it's a little late for that, baby," I whisper, and her eyes widen, nails digging into my skin as tremors ravage her body. She cries out my name as she falls over the edge of her climax. I thrust two more times before I follow her over the edge, moaning her name.

We stay there for a moment, coming down from the high together. Sam's gaze is locked on mine, and more tears begin to fill her eyes. I've never made a girl cry during sex, and I don't think these are tears of pleasure.

"What's wrong?" I ask her as I gently slide out of her, worried that I've hurt her somehow.

"You can't love me, Ryan," Sam says again, letting the tears fall down her cheeks. I recognize the look in her eyes now as her words register. She's afraid.

I gently wipe her cheek and tuck a lock of hair behind her ear. She leans into the touch, closing her eyes.

"Shh, it's okay," I tell her, placing a kiss on her forehead. "Come on, let's get cleaned up," I say, and I hold out my hand as I get off the bed, beckoning her to come with me. I lead us to the bathroom where I start the shower and spend the next twenty minutes gently washing every part of her body as she stares at me with a guarded look. Her silence is frightening, and I replay her words over in my mind as I shut off the shower, and we exit to get dressed.

"You can't love me, Ryan."

Little does she know, I've been in love with Samantha Grace Miller my whole goddamn life.

Chapter Twenty-Four

Sam

I lay next to Ryan, his deep, rhythmic breathing the only thing calming my erratically beating heart. Hours ago, he showed me pleasure that I never knew my body was capable of and devoured me just as he promised. It was perfect, until it wasn't.

I'm haunted by the look of complete infatuation and lust that filled his eyes as he thrusted into me and told me to look at him while he made love to me. My heart stuttered at those words. As much as I desire the type of all-consuming love that I know Ryan could give me, I can't allow it. Ryan can't love me.

Because everyone who loves me dies.

It's that thought that echoes through my mind as I check the time on my phone. It's three in the morning, and my insomnia is back in full force. Worry floods my veins as I think of Annie's impending timeline with Josiah and his obvious threat to Dot's life. Although I just met them, both Dot and Annie's lives hang in limbo under Josiah's hand. Death follows me, and while Annie's situation was already dire, I can't help but wonder if my arrival pushed fate's vengeful hand.

I think of my parents and how I never had the chance to do anything to save them. I couldn't save my mom from cancer, and I couldn't stop my dad's heart from breaking and giving out; if anything, I caused it. The wall of overwhelming grief that's been building up inside of me starts to crumble. That familiar dark fog starts to creep back into my mind, sending me deeper into my thoughts of despair. My muscles buzz with the need for release, craving the distraction of pain. But I can't do that; not here, not now.

There is one thing I can do, though. I can help Annie. I don't know what her plan is, but I'm pretty sure it's going to get her killed. I will not sit by and watch another person in my life be ripped away.

Looking over at Ryan's sleeping form, I check my phone once again and order an uber to the motel. I don't chance changing clothes, afraid of waking Ryan. I know he won't agree with this idea, and I can't risk taking him back to Annie's again. I refuse to let something happen to him.

Sliding out of the bed, I throw my hair into a ponytail and put on my sneakers. I self-consciously tug at my grey pajama shorts and baggy 'grumpy the care-bear' shirt. It was a gift from my dad for my birthday last year, his little humorous jab at my sunny personality and one of my most prized possessions. I carefully grab my phone and wallet before tiptoeing out of the room, silently closing the door behind me.

My phone dings when I make it to the front of the motel letting me know that my uber has arrived. I approach the car, and the older man in the driver's seat eyes me cautiously as he takes in my appearance. I greet him and climb into the backseat, ignoring his questioning gaze.

I confirm the address with him and sit back to watch the dark trees pass us by as we drive to Annie's. Twenty minutes later, I'm exiting the uber and sending the driver off with a gracious tip.

The trailer park is barely lit as I walk up the broken steps of Annie's home. It's a risk to even show up here in the middle of the night, knowing that she's more of a shoot first, ask questions later kind of person. I take a deep breath and knock on the door anyway.

An old truck pulls into the park, and the driver slows as he nears Annie's trailer.

"Hey, sweet thing," the man says out the truck window with a thick southern drawl. "I've got a place you can stay if that's what you're needin'. It won't cost you much." He enunciates the last word, and fear grips my body. I shake my head, refusing to turn and look at him. My palms sweat, and I lift my fist to knock again.

"Fuckin' bitch," the driver spits before hitting the gas and kicking up asphalt as he speeds further into the park.

I knock harder this time, eager to get off this damn doorstep. I hear movement on the other side of the door and breathe a sigh of relief. Then, the door swings open, and I'm suddenly staring at the tip of a gun. Annie's finger hovers over the trigger, and my breathing stops. Then, her eyes widen, and she blinks, lowering the gun.

"Dammit, Sam! I could have shot you!" Annie exclaims. She grabs my wrist and pulls me into the trailer, slamming the door behind us.

"You can't be out there in the middle of the night by yourself! What were you thinking?" She chastises me, and the worry in her voice is so much like my parents that it tugs at my heart. "Where's Ryan? Did he do something?" Annie asks, her grip on the gun instinctively tightening.

"No, no. I just didn't think he'd approve of what I wanted to come here for," I say tentatively. "Could you put that away though?" I ask, nodding to the gun. Annie looks down at her hand and flushes.

"God, I'm sorry. Let me just—," she trails off as she walks over to the tattered couch and sets the gun in her purse on the floor.

"You really shouldn't be here, Sam. It's not safe," Annie says as she sits down on the couch and rests her head in her hands. Her tremors are less severe now, and some of the color has started to return to her skin. She still looks exhausted though, and she's wearing the same outfit from lunch as if she hasn't gone to sleep yet despite it being four in the morning. I suppose fear is its own type of insomnia.

"I came to help you," I say as I walk over and take a seat next to her. She lifts her head from her hands, looking at me in confusion.

"Sam, as much as I appreciate it, I don't think you can help me in this situation," Annie states with a sad smile.

"How much?" I ask.

"What do you mean?" Annie responds, her brows furrowing further.

"How much do you owe Josiah?" I elaborate, and Annie straightens, understanding dawning on her.

"Sam, no—," she begins to object, but I interrupt.

"How much?" I ask again, this time in a sterner tone. Annie lets out an exasperated sigh and looks away from me, guilt creeping into her expression.

"Five grand," she says in a low voice. I take a deep breath in, trying not to let the shock show on my face.

"I'll pay it," I state, and Annie's head snaps in my direction. Her eyes widen and she begins shaking her head.

"Sam, you can't—," she starts, but again, I interject.

"I can. My parents both had life insurance policies that left a remainder for me that was placed in a bank account in my name. Since I'm eighteen I can access it," I explain.

"I can get you the money as soon as the bank opens in a few hours. Maybe that's why I was sent here to find you, so that I could help you now. So that I could keep you safe." My voice falters on the last words as I think of how I couldn't do anything to save my parents. I can do something this time, though.

"Sam, I can't let you do that," Annie whispers, her voice cracking and tears filling her eyes. "They were your parents, honey. You don't owe me anything. I need you to know that," she says, a tear slipping down her cheek.

"My mom and dad were the kindest people I'd ever met, but I always had this loneliness in me that made me more bitter than kind. It wasn't their fault; I just had this darkness inside of me that turned my mind into my own worst enemy," I explain, nervously watching as Annie's eyes track along the scars on my thighs and the healing wound on my wrist. She puts a hand to her mouth and shakes her head.

"I'm so sorry," she says, and I know I was right in assuming that she would blame herself.

"It's not your fault, either. Our minds have failed us both. All we can do now is try to heal. I don't want to be bitter anymore; I want to be kind like my parents. Let me help you, please," I say softly, tears filling my eyes. I know without a doubt that helping Annie would make my parents proud. In a way, they led me to her, and I have to believe it's for this very reason.

"Okay," Annie says reluctantly. I can tell she doesn't want to take any money from me, but she also has no other choice. Not if she wants to keep herself and Dot safe.

"But I have one condition," I say cautiously. I'm not sure how Annie is going to feel about this next part, but she needs help.

"What's that?" Annie asks, skepticism lacing her words.

"After we pay off your debt to Josiah, you have to check yourself into rehab and get help," I tell her, and her face morphs into outright anger.

"No, absolutely not. I'm doing just fine on my own since Josiah cut me off. I don't need some shrink psychoanalyzing my choices and making me feel like some unstable junkie," she says, standing to pace the room. I look around at all the discarded paintings scattered about and the little daises painted into each one. I take a deep breath before standing.

"A daisy can't grow in the dark," I tell her, and she stops pacing to look at me as I approach her.

"You can't stay here and expect to survive when you'll be surrounded by triggers and temptations. Rehab isn't meant to demean you or vilify your choices. It's meant to give you the tools you need to face those triggers and turn away from them rather than giving into the urges," I explain, and my own words begin to resonate with me. Annie still eyes me skeptically, so I continue.

"If you can find the courage to go to rehab and talk to someone, then I can find the courage to get help, too. I don't want to continue giving into my urges that only serve to hurt me, and I don't want you to either," I say truthfully. It would be hypocritical of me to ask her to put aside her pride and get help but not be willing to do the same myself. As hard as it is for me to admit, I think I could benefit from some professional help. I don't want to live a life full of pain and despair.

Annie looks down at the healing burn on my wrist and back up to my face. A tear tracks down her cheek, and the anger disappears from her expression.

"You'll talk to someone?" She asks, her voice quivering. I nod and walk forward, placing my hand on her arm.

"I will if you will. We may not have been able to be there for each other over the last eighteen years, but I'm willing to do what it takes to be here now. Are you?" I ask, a knot forming in my throat. I try to swallow past it, but it grows bigger as Annie nods tearfully and pulls me into her arms.

"I am, little daisy. I'll do whatever it takes," she states, and my arms wrap around her in relief. It feels surreal to be standing here hugging my birth mother, both of us preparing to embark on a healing journey. Wrapped in her arms, I start to think that maybe, just maybe, fate isn't out to get me, and that everything will be okay.

The door to the trailer suddenly opens, and Annie's arms go rigid around me.

"Well, well. If isn't my favorite good Samaritan."

Chapter Twenty-Five

Sam

"Josiah," Annie breathes, stepping in front of me. My heart pounds in my chest as Josiah walks through the door, his lackey following behind him.

"Ronnie," my mind supplies the name Josiah used when speaking of the guy that attacked Ryan and me. My throat constricts when his dark eyes meet mine over Annie's shoulder.

"Well, hello there," Ronnie drawls, eyeing me like a vulture scoping out its next meal. My neck throbs at the memory of his hand choking me as his blade circled my breast. His sleezy grin makes my stomach turn, his obvious unkempt appearance a stark contrast to his suave and handsome counterpart. Despite that, the dark look in Josiah's eyes tells me that Ronnie is the least dangerous of the two.

"What are you doing here, Josiah?" Annie asks, her voice wavering slightly. She's putting on a brave front, but the sweat forming on her hand that's holding my arm gives away her fear.

"I was feeling generous and thought I might stop by and see if we could come to an agreement of sorts," he says, and the smile that he gives Annie sends shivers down my spine. Something tells me that his offer is only going to be beneficial for one of them.

"At four in the morning?" Annie scoffs. Josiah just shrugs as if he didn't just intrude into someone's home in the middle of the night.

"I was in the area, and you know I'm not a fan of being kept waiting. Besides, you used to love when I dropped in unexpectantly," Josiah says, cocking his head to the side and eyeing Annie up and down. If I had any doubts that their relationship was once more than just acquaintances, the look he's giving her now completely expels that doubt.

"That's over, now. Please leave," Annie states, not budging from her spot in front of me. Her protective stance sends a sudden wave of emotions flooding through me, tears prickling my eyes.

"But you haven't even heard my offer," Josiah says. Ronnie rocks on his heels beside him, looking like a coiled snake waiting to strike.

"I don't need to. I'll be paying my debt off today, and then you and I are done," Annie tells him, her tone leaving no room for question. Josiah's eyebrows rise as he taps a finger rhythmically against his leg. His movements are so controlled and calculated that it's unnerving. I'm suddenly finding an odd comfort in the frantic energy radiating off Ronnie. At least there's a predictability to the eagerness for violence in his eyes; with Josiah, I have no idea what he's thinking.

"And how are you doing that?" Josiah asks, his eyes moving from Annie to me. My breathing halts as he takes a step forward, and Annie's grip tightens painfully on my arm. "Another good Samaritan donation? You know this isn't just the cost of a meal or two, sweetheart. Did she tell you how much she owes?"

"I'll get the money. You'll have it today, and then Annie's done. Just like she said," I say shakily. Sweat seeps into my shirt as my heart pounds erratically. Josiah just smirks and shakes his head.

"As nice as that offer is, I've come across a much more lucrative way for Annie to pay off her debt. One that will not only give me the money she owes but also an influx of cash and connections that can't be monetized," Josiah explains, and a new wave of fear settles over me. The excited hunger in Josiah's gaze as he eyes Annie tells me that his mind is made up. Whatever the hell he's about to offer is not going to end well for me or Annie.

"You see," Josiah says, stepping forward again. Annie backs up into me, pulling my body flush against her back. My body trembles against her as the terror in my veins becomes uncontrollable.

"I recently made a friend in Atlanta who makes quite the profit by connecting men with certain needs to beautiful women who need to earn a little extra money," Josiah explains, and my stomach turns. Oh God, this cannot be happening.

"Now, I've already promised my new friend that I have a lovely woman that has a debt to pay off who could really bring him in a desirable profit." Josiah steps into Annie's space, his eyes looking intently into hers before looking at me with that same hunger. Something shifts then in his expression, and overwhelming horror sweeps through me.

"But I suppose I never did tell him who I was bringing, only that she would produce quite a profit. And sweetheart," he says, his attention completely on me now as he licks his bottom lip appreciatively. "I think you could be the gift that keeps on giving."

"No," Annie growls, her hand gripping my arm painfully. "You'll get your money and that's it. No more deals." Her voice is laced with terror, and a sob nearly escapes me.

Josiah smiles and shakes his head. "How about one more offer? You let me take your pretty little friend here to my guy in Atlanta, and I'll consider your debt paid. I'll also count her payment for your future purchases from me," Josiah offers, grinning wickedly at Annie. My heart stops beating as sweat coats my body.

I'm not a fucking piece of property to be bartered and sold. I want to say as much, but fear stops the words from leaving my mouth. I don't know how to get out of this situation without me or Annie getting hurt, and the way Annie's back goes rigid against me tells me she's thinking the same thing.

"What do you say, Annie bear? You'll keep your access to my supply of pills, clear your debt, and it won't cost you a thing. Well, except your daughter." His mischievous grin widens as he takes in mine and Annie's mirrored expressions.

"What, you thought I wouldn't ask around? Dot's been talking all over town about the return of her beautiful granddaughter. What was it she called you? Oh, her little daisy," Josiah states with sickening enunciation. The nickname feels completely vile and unsettling coming from his mouth.

"Don't," Annie snarls, anger dripping from the single word. Josiah just laughs, and Ronnie rocks on his heels in anticipation.

"Come on, Annie, we both know you were never meant to be a mother. Don't start trying to be one now. You've given her up once before, so what's one more time? At least you'll get something out of the deal this time around." Josiah's words slice through me, eviscerating my soul.

Without even trying, he's reaching into my mind and pulling my greatest fears and darkest thoughts to the surface. I've never felt as if I fit into the world around me, always feeling instead like a secondary being taking up too much space. Now, Josiah wants Annie to solidify those thoughts and fears by abandoning me again and selling me off to the highest bidder.

The darkness in my mind creeps in from the edges as I wait for Annie to say something. Her back is still rigid against me, her hand still gripping me tightly. Josiah eyes her with a mischievous intensity, and then he winks as if seeing something in her gaze that he approves of.

Annie's grip loosens on my arm, and my heart stops. There's no way she's considering this, right? I hold my breath as Annie's hand falls away from my arm, and she takes a step away from me. My soul fractures into a thousand pieces as betrayal shoots through me. This can't be happening. How could I have been so wrong about the woman in front of me?

"Over my dead body," Annie snarls. Relief floods my system, and I almost cry out. Before I can say or do anything, though, Josiah's smile drops, and violence etches into his features. Suddenly, Annie rears back and spits in Josiah's face. I gasp, and Josiah's hand shoots up with a violent cracking sound. The impact sends Annie collapsing to the floor, a cry escaping her.

"That can be arranged," Josiah states calmly while wiping the spit from his face. "Grab her," he commands Ronnie, and my body freezes. Ronnie's been waiting for this moment since he arrived, and he doesn't hesitate. He lunges at me, and I try to force myself to move, but fear roots me in place.

Just as Ronnie closes in on my frozen form, Annie's leg kicks out, sending him careening to the floor. Ronnie crashes into a pile of discarded paintings, and like a coward, I jump over him and bolt for the door. I make it three steps before Josiah's hand shoots out and latches onto my ponytail. He snatches me back and hurls me into the nearby wall. I shriek as I land with a sickening crunch and scream as pain explodes through my left wrist.

"Sam!" Annie screams, jumping up to rush toward me. Ronnie cuts into her path, and I sob, writhing in pain as he grabs her by the throat and throws her down onto the floor. Annie cries out, and I push myself up to my knees, desperately trying to get to her. Annie attempts to get up, but Ronnie slams his foot into her stomach, sending her sprawling back onto the floor. She moans in pain, and I cradle my wrist as I try to crawl toward her.

My head is suddenly snatched back again, and I shriek as Josiah's deep voice fills the space next to me.

"Watch this," he says as his grip holds me in place, my eyes trained on the scene in front of me. Annie tries to get up again, but Ronnie advances on her. Just as Annie gets her feet under her and turns around, a flash of silver appears in Ronnie's hand.

"MOM!" I scream with every fiber of my being as Ronnie strikes out, thrusting the switchblade into Annie's abdomen. She doesn't even cry out, her mouth just parts in shock as Ronnie yanks the blade back out. I scream as Annie's legs buckle. She grabs at her stomach, and her hands grow red with blood as she stumbles and collapses to the floor.

Rage floods my veins as Josiah laughs in my ear. The wicked sound propels me as I gather all my strength and slam my elbow back into his face. A revolting crunch is followed by a roar of pain as Josiah releases my hair and falls back to grasp at his bleeding nose. I don't hesitate when I see Ronnie turn from Annie to advance on me. I propel myself the few feet over to the couch, falling next to it, and thrust my hand into Annie's purse.

In one swift motion, I pull out the gun, release the safety, turn, and pull the trigger. The deafening bang echoes through the trailer as the bullet hits home. Ronnie stumbles back, swaying in shock as blood begins to spread across the chest of his white shirt. He crumples to the floor just as Josiah stands and rushes at me.

I swing the gun at him and fire. The bullet strikes his arm, and he stumbles back with a curse.

"You fucking bitch," he snarls through gritted teeth, spit flying out of his mouth. "I'm going to kill you."

"Take one more step," I begin, training the gun on his head. "And the next one goes through your skull."

Josiah snarls, gripping his bleeding arm just feet away from me. Annie moans and makes a terrifying gurgling noise as blood soaks the floor from her wound. Ronnie lays lifeless next to her, and Josiah eyes his prone form, considering his next move.

A truck door slams loudly outside, echoing through the trailer. I startle, the gun shaking in my hand, and I almost drop it at the next sound I hear.

"Samantha!" Ryan yells from the front porch, obvious anger and concern in his tone. Josiah looks at the front door and then back to me.

"This isn't fucking over," he snarls. Blood soaks his hand as he moves carefully to the back door through the kitchen. He doesn't turn his back on me, and I keep the gun trained on his retreating form. Something keeps me from pulling the trigger, and I'm not sure if it's revulsion at the idea of taking another life or fear that I'll miss, and he'll just kill me and Ryan anyways.

"Yes, it is," I state as he opens the back door and exits with a curse. The front door flies open at the same time, and Ryan storms in as I breathe a sigh of relief. I drop the gun and stumble over to Annie, falling to my knees next to her. Her eyes are barely open, and blood covers her shirt.

"Sam—," Ryan begins but stops short when he takes in the growing puddle of warm liquid that soaks my knees and the two bodies lying on the floor.

"Help me," I cry as I rip my t-shirt off, leaving myself in a bra and shorts, and press it against Annie's abdomen. Blinding pain flares through my wrist as I apply pressure, and a scream escapes me, but I don't let up.

"Shit," Ryan curses, stumbling forward while removing his own shirt. He presses it on top of mine, Annie's blood already soaking the fabrics. Ryan uses one hand to add pressure to my own and grabs his phone with the other.

He dials quickly and then sets the phone down next to us. His eyes meet mine, and I want so badly to just fall into the safety of his arms.

"9-1-1, where's your emergency?" A voice says through the speaker, and I'm thrown back to that same sound piercing through the haze of grief as I laid across my father's dead body just days ago. Ryan's response muffles in my ears as I look down at Annie and press against her wound. She moans, her eyes fluttering as she teeters on the edge of consciousness. I lean over, and my tears fall onto her face, mixing with her own.

"Please don't leave me," I sob, and Annie's hand lifts just enough to caress my cheek. Her fingers and lips are paling, and her touch is growing colder. Her face morphs into the images of my mother and father lying dead before me, and I sob uncontrollably.

"Little daisy," she whispers, and then her eyes flutter closed, her hand falling away from my face. Sirens blare as they grow closer outside, but I barely hear them over the sound of my own screams.

Chapter Twenty-Six

Ryan

"I'm going to kill her." The words repeated over and over in my head when I woke up suddenly to an empty bed and silent room, not a hint of Sam in sight. Her phone, shoes, and wallet were missing, and while my keys were still there, I had no doubt that she had found a way to get to Annie's house. That was the only explanation for her absence; she had thought of some way to help Annie and had assumed I would try to talk her out of it.

Well, she was damn right. I didn't drive her all the way up here just to watch her get herself hurt, and putting herself in the middle of Annie's situation cannot possibly end well. I was in my truck in a matter of moments, calling Sam's phone, and cursing every time it went straight to voicemail. An uneasy feeling settled in my gut as the roar of the truck's engine broke the silence of the darkness around me.

I don't know what the hell she was thinking going over there in the middle of the night.

I broke every speed limit and arrived at the trailer park in record time. Nothing prepared me, however, for the gunshot that rang through the air as I pulled in. I sped up to Annie's lot, one of the only ones with lights on, and jumped out of the truck with my heart in my throat.

"Samantha!" I yelled, fear catapulting me up the broken steps and through the front door. Her name was passing through my lips again when I halted, a scene of crimson and death greeting me. Sam was on her knees in a rapidly growing puddle of blood, Annie laid out next to her. The guy that ambushed us a few days ago was on the floor as well, but his frozen form and unblinking eyes told me he wasn't a threat anymore.

Before I could comprehend the scene in front of me, Sam was ripping her shirt off and pressing her hands into Annie's bleeding abdomen.

"Help me," Sam cried as she applied pressure, a scream of pain ripping from her chest. As I rushed over, I could see the swollen and rapidly bruising nature of Sam's wrist. It was obviously broken, and I had to tamper down my boiling rage as I pulled my own shirt off and pressed it on top of Sam's.

Pulling my phone out, I called 9-1-1 and relayed the necessary details, an eerie feeling of déjà vu falling over me. Minutes later though, Sam was screaming as Annie fell unconscious. I had to physically pull her off Annie when the paramedics arrived and forced her into my truck while the police followed us to the hospital.

Now, I stand next to Sam in the small ER room, both of us dressed in grey sweats that the police provided us with when they took our clothes as evidence. I watch as the doctor puts the cast on Sam's arm, the x-ray having shown a clean break in her wrist.

"And why were you at Ms. Mason's home so early in the morning?" The officer standing next to the doctor questions. Sam grits her teeth as the doctor applies the pink fabric over the cast plaster.

"I wanted to offer her my help. She was in a tough predicament with Josiah, and I knew I could help," Sam explains, and the officer eyes her wearily. His nametag reads Sgt. Bradley, and his demeanor is nothing short of dismissive and intimidating.

"What about the bruising on your neck? That isn't from tonight," he states, pointing to Sam's bruised skin. My fists clench at my side as he glances accusatorily at me.

"We had a run-in with Ronnie a couple of days ago when we first went to Annie's," Sam explains in an exasperated tone, and the cop tilts his head at her.

"So, you had previously established motive to want to shoot him?" Officer Bradley asks as he writes something down in his notepad. Sam straightens, and I step closer to her, my whole body on edge.

"What? No! I was already at Annie's when he and Josiah barged in. They attacked us when Annie wouldn't agree to his demands," Sam huffs out angrily.

"And what were his demands?" Officer Bradley questions as the doctor finishes the cast and exits the room with a simple nod. Sam glances anxiously at me before turning back to the officer to answer.

"He wanted Annie to agree to let him take me to a guy in Atlanta… to sell me." Sam mutters the last part softly, but I hear her loud and clear. Violent rage barrels through me with dangerous intensity.

"What the fuck?!" I exclaim, and Sam flinches at the sudden outburst. I close my eyes and pinch my nose, trying to calm the roaring anger within me.

"Sir, if can't compose yourself, I'm going to need you to leave," Officer Bradley states without even looking at me. He just continues writing on his notepad, and Sam reaches out to grab my hand with her uninjured one.

"I'm sorry, sir," I say as I caress my thumb over the back of Sam's hand, trying to ground myself in her touch.

"Did he say this friend's name?" Bradley asks, and Sam shakes her head.

"No, he never said. Just that he had promised to bring him a woman who could bring in a large profit," she explains.

"So, he makes this offer to Annie, and she what, refuses?" The officer questions with a disbelieving tone.

"Yes, she refused," Sam bites out. "And then, he told Ronnie to grab me, and all hell broke loose."

"That's when that happened?" He asks, nodding to Sam's arm cast. Sam nods as a pained look crosses her face.

"Yeah. He, uh, grabbed me by my hair and threw me into the wall. I landed on my wrist and heard a snap. Before I could do anything, he gripped me by the hair again and forced me to watch as Ronnie stabbed Annie."

I fist my hand not holding Sam's so tightly that my nails break through the skin of my palm. I've never felt this much rage, even on the days that my father beat me so badly I couldn't see straight.

"I elbowed Josiah in the face as hard as I could and lunged for Annie's purse where I knew she kept her gun. I pulled it out just as Ronnie came at me with the knife in his hand. It was self-defense." Annie enunciates the last words, giving Bradley a hard stare.

"And Josiah? You said on the scene that you shot him as well, but he ran off." Sam nods and swallows loudly.

"Yeah, he saw Ronnie go down and came at me. I shot him through the arm and told him not to come near me. He heard Ryan pull up outside, and he left out the back door." Guilt settles in my stomach at Sam's words. If only I'd woken up sooner, gotten there quicker, maybe I could have stopped all of this.

"And you just let him leave?" Bradley asks, his tone filled

disbelief again.

"I didn't want to hurt anyone else," Sam says softly. Her hand trembles in mine as tears fill her eyes.

"Well, you won't be able to see Ms. Mason until I can get a statement from her as well and ensure that hers corroborates yours. If it doesn't, then I'll be seeing you again real soon, Ms. Miller," Bradley states smugly as he tucks away his notepad and walks out.

Sam barely blinks as Officer Bradley leaves, just stares at the floor with a haunted look. That cold fear settles into my veins again that only occurs when Sam gets in these dissociative states. I'm not sure how to pull her out, and not knowing how Annie's surgery is going isn't helping.

They rushed her back for emergency surgery when we got here, but they warned us that it would be touch and go for a while.

"Hey," I say softly as I crouch down in front of Sam. Her bright blues eyes look up at me, and the despair in them has me dropping to my knees. I rest my hands on her legs, the small touch anchoring me to her, reminding me that she's here. "Are you hurt anywhere else?"

Sam just shakes her head, fresh tears prickling in her eyes. I lift one of my hands up to cup her cheek, my thumb caressing her skin in soothing strokes.

"Hey, you're okay. It's going to be okay. Annie's in surgery, and we've already determined that she's one hell of a fighter. Do you really think she's going to let a piece of shit like Ronnie do her in?" I ask, feeling the truth in my words as I speak. Sam shakes her head softly, a small smile forming on her lips.

"Hell no," she whispers, and the sound thaws some of that cold fear in my veins.

"Now," I say, standing and stepping into her space. She looks up at my towering frame as I rest my hands on either side of her, boxing her in. "What the fuck were you thinking?"

Sam grimaces, guilt creeping into her expression. She darts her gaze away from mine, refusing to look me in the eyes.

"I'm sorry, I didn't think things would go that way. I just wanted to help her, and I thought you would try to talk me out of it," she says, and I reach out to gently grab her chin, turning her head to meet my gaze.

"You're damn right I would have, because helping her means putting yourself in Josiah's crosshairs. I never would have brought you here if I knew it meant throwing you right in the middle of danger. I understand your desire to help her; she's your birth mother, and she's in a desperate situation. But your life, Samantha," I say, gripping her chin a little tighter, her eyes widening and lips parting. "Is non-negotiable. So, the next time you feel like throwing yourself to the wolves, you better drag me right along with you, because life without you is not an option. It never has been. Do you understand?"

Sam pulls in a shaky breath, and tears brim in her eyes.

"You can't mean that," she says lowly, fear saturating her words.

"With every fiber of my being," I state firmly. "I've never felt about anyone the way that I feel about you, and I wouldn't want to wake up everyday and not have your beautiful face be the first thing I think about."

Sam's skin trembles under my touch, and she shakes her head.

"Don't say that," she breathes pleadingly. My heart breaks at her palpable fear, and I grip her chin tighter, my gaze boring into hers.

"Say what? That I've been in love with you since the first time I watched you climb out of your bedroom window just to sit under the tree and sketch beneath the moonlight when you were thirteen? Baby, my life has been yours for far longer than you realize," I tell her, leaning in so that my breath ghosts across her lips. Her chin quivers between my fingers, and a tear slides down her cheek.

"Please, don't love me, Ryan," she whispers, and my heart stutters at the pain in her voice.

"I don't have a choice, Samantha. Tell me why you're fighting it," I say, caressing her bottom lip with my thumb. A shiver runs through her, and I know she feels this electricity between us, yet she's keeping me at arm's length.

"Because everyone who loves me dies," she admits, her tears falling in rapid succession now. Grief rips at my heart as the weight of her words hit me. It's why she looked so scared when leaving Dot's house and why she snuck out to Annie's in the middle of the night. She's terrified of loving and losing another person, but death is the curse of life.

"If loving you is my damnation, then sentence me to death. Not loving you would kill me anyways, and I promise that death would be torturously slow and painful." I know my words are intense, but everything I've ever felt for Sam has been intense. I've loved her from afar for years, and now that I've truly seen every part of her, I'll never be able to look away.

"You don't mean that," Sam says, shaking her head. I release her chin to cup her face and wipe at her tears.

"I've never meant anything more," I state with conviction. "I love you, Samantha." The words feel like a cathartic release, finally laying claim to the feelings that have lived inside of me for so long. Sam inhales sharply and holds her breath as if letting the words settle with the air in her lungs. She blinks, releases a breath, and then lunges for me. Her body collides against mine, and I close my eyes, falling into her touch. Our tongues meet in a kiss of sweet surrender as I cradle her face in my hands.

Sam pulls away first, her lips staying within an inch of mine as her eyes stare into my own. The look of pure vulnerability and fear in them makes my heart clench, and I tighten my hold on her face, refusing to let her go. Whatever she sees in my eyes causes her to release another shaky breath.

"Will you let me love you?" I ask breathlessly. "Let me show you that you're worth the risk," I say as I wipe a tear from her cheek. Sam trembles beneath my touch, and a sob escapes her as she nods once. I pull her into my chest and kiss the top of her head as she breaks down in my arms.

"You're worth loving, Samantha," I whisper, her arms wrapping around me tightly, holding me like a lifeline. I hold her until her sobs turn to sniffles, and a knock sounds on the door. We pull away from each other as Annie's surgeon enters the room. I hold my breath, trying to decipher his unreadable expression.

"She's going to be okay," he says with a smile. "We were able to repair the artery, and there was no damage to any of her organs. She's lucky you were there to keep her from bleeding out. You saved her life," he says, and Sam collapses back onto the edge of the ER bed.

"Thank you," she breathes, and the doctor nods with a grin. "She'll be moved to a room for observation for the next 48 hours, then she can go home. It's going to be a long road for her, though, since she can only have over the counter pain meds. She'll need a strong support system."

"I'll make sure she gets that," Sam states with a stern nod. The doctor tells us that someone will come to get us once Annie's in her room, and then he leaves.

I gather Sam in my arms, pressing her against my chest again.

"I've got you. It's going to be okay," I murmur as her tears of relief soak into my shirt. "She's going to be okay."

Chapter Twenty-Seven

Sam

Hours after the disaster at Annie's, I'm finally allowed to see her. I waited anxiously outside of her room as she came to and gave Officer Bradley her statement. He came out and cast me a narrowed look before telling me that our statements matched, and they'd be on the lookout for Josiah.

Now, I push open the hospital room door with a sweaty palm and step inside. Annie sits up against the pillows, her skin pale and eyes hooded. Her hand rests on her stomach, the hospital gown making her thin body look frailer. She grimaces in pain but tries to mask it with a smile as I step closer to the bed.

"Sam," she breathes softly. My heart constricts at the single word, and I almost start sobbing.

"Are you okay?" I ask in a shaky voice. Emotion clogs my throat, and tears start to cloud my vision. Annie nods and reaches out to touch the cast on my arm.

"I'm fine, little daisy. I'm so sorry this happened," she states with a shake of her head. "You should have never been in danger." Annie's voice breaks more with each word.

"I'm glad I was there," I say honestly. "Who knows what would have happened if Josiah had been able to take you like he planned." I shake my head at the reminder that either one of us could have been taken and sent to a truly horrific fate.

"You were so strong, my little daisy. You saved my life," Annie says with tears in her eyes. An invisible weight falls off my shoulder, and I nearly collapse in relief. She's here; she's safe. I didn't lose anyone else.

"I just found you," I begin shakily. "There's no way I was letting you go."

"Oh, Sam," Annie whispers as tears slide down her cheek. The door opens then, and Dot barrels through with Ryan following in her wake.

"Annie Mason! Don't you ever scare me like that again!" Dot quickly moves across the room and leans over the bed to throw her arms around her daughter. Annie grimaces in pain at the movement but immediately sinks into her mother's embrace.

"Mama, I'm so sorry," Annie says with a sob. Dot just presses her head against her chest and shushes her.

"It's okay, sweet girl. You're going to be okay," Dot murmurs in that soothing voice of hers. She pulls back after a moment and turns to look at me.

"My little daisy. Are you okay?" She asks as she moves to embrace me. I fall into her touch, letting her warmth and safety envelop me. Something about her hugs heals an ache that lives deep in my soul.

"I'm okay," I murmur back, burying my face into her shoulder and just breathing in her scent. She smells like cotton and lavender, the perfect combination of comfort and home.

Dot pulls back and cups my face in her hands, her gaze searching mine.

"I didn't know what to think when Ryan showed up on my

doorstep without you. My God, I was so worried," she says and yanks me against her again. I bask in the embrace until I pull away to scan the room for Ryan. I spot him standing in the corner, his arms crossed in a stiff posture as he watches us. I step away from Dot as she turns back to Annie and move toward him.

"Thank you for going to pick her up," I say softly. Ryan nods and pulls my hand into his.

"Of course," he states, his eyes roaming over every inch of my body as if cataloging every detail.

"Everything alright?" I ask as I take in his dark gaze. He nods to Annie and Dot before responding.

"Why don't we go grab a coffee and give them some time to talk?" I nod and then turn back to Dot and Annie.

"We are going to go grab a coffee. Do you guys want anything?" I offer, but they both shake their heads. A few moments later, Ryan and I head down the hall, hand in hand. There's a palpable energy radiating off him that I can't quite pinpoint.

We approach the elevators of the empty quiet hall, but Ryan keeps moving past them with a tug on my hand.

"The elevators—" I begin, but Ryan interrupts.

"No," he states, his grip tightening on my hand. Confusion fills me as we round a corner and head for the stairs. Right before we get to the stair entrance, however, Ryan opens a supply closet door and yanks us both inside.

"What are you—" I start, but stop as Ryan closes the closet door, shrouding us in darkness. I watch as he grabs as nearby vacuum and braces it under the door handle, locking it in place.

"Ryan," I whisper, afraid of someone hearing us. He whirls on me in the darkness and storms toward me, backing me into a shelf of cleaning supplies.

"Shh," he commands lowly as his hand covers my mouth. Heat floods my system as his body presses into mine. My back digs painfully into the shelf as Ryan grinds against me. I relish the pain, and moan against his hand.

Ryan presses his hand harder against my mouth to muffle the sound as his other hand slides down my stomach and into the waistband of my sweatpants. His fingers instantly press against my wet pussy and slide through my center. My eyes roll at the contact, and I buck my hips, pushing his fingers deeper into me.

Ryan adds another finger, and the pressure is intoxicating as he thrusts them in and out. I'm on the edge of shattering in ecstasy when his fingers pause inside of me, and his thumb presses roughly against my clit. I groan in frustration and try to grind against his hand to create that desperate friction. Ryan keeps his other hand pressed against my mouth as he leans down to press his lips against my ear.

"You will never put yourself in danger like that again, do you understand?" He growls, and the words send shivers down my spine and heat to my core. One thing I'm learning about Ryan is that he cares abundantly and protects fiercely. Leaving him in that motel room to go to Annie's in the middle of the night completely robbed him of his primary instinct to protect the people he loves.

And he loves me. His words from the emergency room ring through my mind as he presses his fingers deeper, and I cry against his hand. My hips try to circle his fingers to chase the orgasm I had been so close to moments ago.

"You will never compromise your life again, do you understand?" He growls again, his words almost sending me over the edge. I nod desperately against his hand and moan as he kisses my neck while moving his thumb to circle my clit.

"Good girl, now cum for me," Ryan commands as he thrusts his fingers in and out at a dizzying pace. His thumb presses into my clit, and I shatter around him as tremors of pleasure wrack my body.

"Mmm, good girl," he purrs as he pulls out of me and brings his wet fingers to his lips. He drops his other hand from my mouth, and I gape at him as he sucks my orgasm from his fingers.

"Delicious," Ryan states with a wink. I stand there frozen as he adjusts my sweatpants for me and moves to the door. He removes the vacuum from under the handle and turns back to me.

"Come on, we better go get those coffees," Ryan says casually and holds his hand out to me. I shakily grab it and let him lead us out of the closet. My face heats as I scan the hallway for witnesses but see none.

Ryan seems to detect my embarrassment and lets go of my hand to throw his arm around my shoulders, pulling me closer to his side. He kisses the side of my head as we walk to the elevators, and I relax into the touch. I glance up at him and realize just how at ease he seems now compared to how he seemed in Annie's room earlier.

He didn't even chase his own pleasure in the storage closet, just brought me to the heights of bliss while showing me just how much my life means to him.

As Ryan leads us to the coffee shop downstairs and orders my iced hazelnut latte without even needing to ask, I take in every angle of his face and the dimple in his cheek. God, I want to stare into those stormy eyes every day for the rest of my life.

Fear settles in my stomach as that thought crosses my mind. I'm falling for him, and I'm fucking terrified.

Chapter Twenty-Eight

Sam

Two days later, Annie is released from the hospital. Ryan and I spent the last couple of days packing her small collection of clothes, paintings, and necessities, and moving them over to Dot's. It was painful to be back in the space where Annie nearly bled out, and Ronnie died at my hand. Ryan's presence kept me anchored as we packed her things, keeping me from slipping back into a dissociative traumatized state.

I hold Annie's arm now, Ryan on her other side, as we climb the steps of Dot's house. The door flies open and Dot dashes out, throwing her arms around Annie and me, leaving Ryan hanging awkwardly off to the side. The warmth and safety of her embrace is like the beacon of a lighthouse calling us home.

"My sweet girls. Welcome home," Dot says, the softness of her voice settling over my soul like a soothing balm.

"I'm so sorry, Mama," Annie says softly as she wraps her arms around her mother. I know she feels like an imposition to be coming back home after all these years, but we all refuse to let her go back to the trailer.

"This is your home, Annie. You can always come back to it," Dot says. She releases us and places a warm hand on my cheek. "And you, too, sweet girl. This is your home, too." Her words and touch bring tears to my eyes as I nod softly.

"Come on, I've got some lunch ready for us," Dot states as she turns to usher us inside.

We follow Dot through the house and into the kitchen that's filled with a delicious smell. Ryan helps Annie into her chair as I help Dot plate the food. I pass her bowls as she scoops the beef and veggies into them and looks at me with deep appreciation.

"Annie told me you convinced her to check into rehab. I can't thank you enough for that, Sam. You've given us both the strength to heal, but I hope you've saved some of that strength for yourself, too." She looks pointedly at me, and a small smile plays on my lips.

"I think I have," I say as I turn to look back at Ryan who sits with Annie at the table discussing the paintings that hang on the walls.

"Not just your heart, little daisy," Dot states as she sets down the bowl to reach out and tap against the burn scar on my right wrist. My heart stutters at the contact as embarrassment and shame flood my body. "Your mind, too."

"I—I'm going to talk to someone," I state nervously. Dot nods as she passes me a full bowl.

"Good, now let's eat," Dot says casually, not an ounce of disappointment or judgement in her expression. She turns and carries two bowls to the table while I grab the other two. I set one in front of Ryan and take the seat next to him. He smiles up at me, that damned dimple making butterflies flutter in my stomach. That overwhelming fear of my feelings for him settles over me again.

I look away from him and focus on the vase of fresh flowers sitting at the center of the table. They're colorful daisies and tulips bathed in the sunlight coming from the large kitchen windows. They remind me of my mother and the flowers Ryan used to bring for her. God, even the flowers bring my thoughts back to him.

Annie sits nervously in her chair as Dot places the bowl of roast, potatoes, and carrots in front of her. I reach my hand across the table and place it on top of Annie's, sweeping my thumb across the back of her hand in comforting strokes. My other arm throbs in its cast, a constant reminder that Josiah is still out there. I refuse to think of him right now, though.

"Hey, it's going to be okay. You're moving in the right direction, and that's all you can do," I tell her, trying to ease her nerves. We are scheduled to take her to the rehab facility this evening, and I can't imagine how terrified she must be. While it's only for thirty days, I can only assume it will feel like an eternity for her.

"I just don't know what the future will look like," Annie begins. "I haven't lived with my mother since I was eighteen and haven't held a steady job my entire life. How in the world am I supposed to manage doing anything normal while trying not to relapse?" Annie's voice is shaky as her leg bounces up and down under the table. Dot eyes her with concern but doesn't say anything.

"I called Grace," I begin. "She's the adoption agency worker that handled my adoption, though I doubt you remember her. Well, she has a friend who works with recovering parents to reintegrate into everyday life. She sets them up with AA meetings and a sponsor, and she can help you find a job that works well for you. I've already reached out to her and given her your information. She and Dot will be the ones to pick you up from the recovery center next month," I explain. There's a nervousness in my voice, and I'm afraid Annie will think I've overstepped here. I don't want to steamroll her into recovery, but I want to help in any way that I can.

"Oh, Sam. You didn't have to do all that," Annie says, placing her hand on top of mine. Tears shine in her eyes as she speaks again.

"You are so much more than I deserve."

"That's not true. You can do this; I just need you to try for me, okay?" I tell her, knowing that this is, without a doubt, one of the hardest things she's ever done. Annie just nods, visibly swallowing the lump in her throat and holding her tears at bay.

"Okay, enough of that. Let's dig in before it gets cold," Dot says, reminding us of the steaming bowls of roast in front of us. It smells divine, and as we dig in, the robust flavor suddenly reminds me of my father's cooking. His memory settles over me as I look around the table. It's strange to recognize that his death is the catalyst that brought me to this moment. Grief wars with the feeling of home that fills me as I take in the faces around me.

Ryan digs into his bowl, moaning and shoveling large spoonfuls into his mouth. I try to swallow past the sudden lump in my throat as I remember the bitterness I would feel sitting across the table from Ryan at family dinners over the years. All he wanted was a hot meal in a safe space, and I went out of my way to make it a hostile environment each time.

Somehow, throughout it all, he fell in love with me. My vision clouds at the memory of him telling me those words while he held me in the ER. I blink away the tears, trying to tamper down the fear that overwhelms my system. Letting him love me is dangerous but loving him back would be utterly fatal. How would I survive if I gave him all the pieces of me just for him to decide I'm too broken to ever be enough for him? Loving him could mean losing him, and the pieces of me would just crumble to nothingness.

"Sam, I've been thinking," Dot interrupts my spiraling thoughts, looking between me and Annie. "How would you like to come here for Thanksgiving and Christmas this year? Ryan you'd be welcome as well, you'll just have to sleep on the couch, of course," Dot states with a knowing grin that has heat growing across my cheeks. I look to Ryan who grins wildly at me and then turn back to my grandmother.

"We'd love that, Maw Maw," I say with a pounding heart. Dot gasps sharply, her wrinkled hand coming up to rest on her chest.

"Oh, my sweet girl." Tears fill her eyes, and Annie reaches over to hold her mother's hand. "Nothing would make me happier."

"I'm so sorry I robbed us of so many years," Annie says sadly, and I shake my head.

"You didn't. You gave me the chance to love and be loved by two amazing parents, and they led me right back to you."

Annie just nods, tears silently falling down her cheeks. Ryan's hand comes to rest on my thigh, giving me a reassuring squeeze. I try to ignore the butterflies and fear that settle in my stomach at his touch.

An hour later, our bags are in the truck, and Annie is wrapped in Dot's tight embrace.

"You go in there and let them help you, and then you come back to me. Got it?" Dot says as she hugs Annie.

"I will, Mama. I love you," Annie states, kissing Dot on the cheek. Then she pulls away, wipes her tears, and climbs into the backseat of Ryan's truck. Ryan hugs Dot, and she whispers something in his ear that has his cheeks turning red. He clears his throat and nods to her before getting into the driver's seat. She watches him go with a grin as I step forward to wrap my arms around her.

Her warmth envelops me, and I don't think I'll ever get enough of her hugs.

"My little daisy," Dot murmurs into my ear. "You are my most beautiful blessing."

Her words strangle me with emotion. I inhale her cotton and lavender smell, reminding me of my mom. Dot feels like a bridge between my two worlds, someone who reminds me of home, whether it be her space or the one I grew up in. My emotions feel safe with her, like I can be and feel however, and she won't judge.

She makes me feel as though it's safe to love and be loved.

I try to focus on that thought as she holds me tightly in her embrace. I'm terrified to love her because my love is a curse, but I'm already falling so deep into her warmth and safety. Loving her is inevitable.

"Call me anytime you want, little daisy," Dot says, and I nod against her shoulder.

"I'll call you every day," I promise, knowing that I will crave the sound of her soothing voice.

We pull apart, and she places a kiss to my cheek. I bite my cheek to keep the tears from escaping my eyes.

"Thank you," she whispers. "You brought my Annie back to me and fulfilled my greatest dream. You, my granddaughter, deserve all the love in the world. Don't hold yourself back from it," she says, giving me a knowing look.

I cast a glance back at Ryan in the truck and swallow nervously.

"I'll try," I say honestly, and I throw my arms around Dot for one more hug. I kiss her on the cheek before climbing into the passenger seat. We wave goodbye as Ryan pulls the truck out of the driveway and navigates us to the highway.

Forty minutes later, we arrive at the rehab facility where Annie will stay for the next month. Her leg bounces with anxiety in the backseat, and she bites her lip as she takes in the view of the large building. There are plants lining the entrance and a water fountain with benches next to it off to the side. It's a beautiful estate that is going to cost me a large portion of the money in my account, but I know my dad would be proud of the way I'm choosing to spend it.

We park and exit the truck, and Ryan grabs Annie's bag from the back. I grab her hand and nod, silently telling her that it's going to be okay. Hand in hand, we walk inside and get her checked in. We follow the attendee as he leads us to Annie's spacious room that overlooks the fountain outside. Annie eyes the space wearily, and though it's a nicer space than she had before, I know it doesn't feel like home.

"Your daughter mentioned you like to paint, so we brought a few of our art supplies up to your room for you," he says, pointing to the small collection of canvases, paint, and brushes in the corner of the room. Annie turns to see the supplies, and her eyes light up, tears forming. Relief washes over me at her excitement. At least she will have one thing here to bring her a piece of happiness and home over the next month.

"Oh, this is wonderful. Thank you," she says as she runs her fingers over the blank canvases. The attendee nods and exits, giving us space to say our goodbyes. Annie looks at me with a vulnerable expression that has me pulling her into my arms, careful of her still healing wound.

"I'm so proud of you," I tell her, and her arms tighten around me.

"Oh, Sam. You are my most perfect creation," she says, pulling back to cup my cheek with her hand. Then, she reaches into her back pocket and hands me a slip of paper.

"While I was in the hospital, I made a few calls to some old friends. I was able to find out where your birth father is living now." My heart stops as I eye the folded paper. The name of the other person who created me is on this paper, but I can't bring myself to look.

"This is his name and address, and it's yours to do as you please. I'm so sorry I robbed you both of the opportunity to know each other all these years," she states, her voice wavering.

"You found him. You didn't have to do that," I say in disbelief. I can only imagine how hard it was for Annie to reach out to the people of her rocky past when she was in the middle of recovering from a stab wound and addiction. She did that for me, though.

"I would do anything for you, my little daisy." Her voice is loving and kind as she reaches out a hand to touch my cheek.

With a trembling hand, I slide the folded paper into my back pocket and throw my arms around Annie.

"Thank you," I say, and there's so much more I want to tell her and so many more things I want to know about her, but right now, we both need to focus on healing.

"Take care of my girl," Annie says to Ryan as we pull apart. He nods and smiles at her.

"I've got Sam, you just take care of yourself, okay?" He states and pulls Annie into a small side hug. Then, he moves back to my side and takes my hand in his. There's such a naturalness and ease to the way that Dot and Annie entrust my safety to Ryan. It sets off the butterflies in my stomach again.

"See you soon, okay?" I tell Annie and blow her a kiss before leaving. If I don't force myself to leave now, I'm afraid I never will. Ryan's grip on my hand calms my erratically beating heart as we walk to the truck.

"She'll be okay," he says, opening my door for me. I look up at his handsome face and stormy blue eyes that I want so desperately to fall into.

"I know," I begin, and reach up to touch his cheek. He leans into my touch, and I'm reminded of Dot's words. I deserve to heal and let myself love and be loved. I don't want to continue keeping everyone at arm's length until I die alone and miserable.

If Ryan's willing to risk the curse of loving me, then perhaps I can chance stepping out of the darkness to love him. I stand up on my tiptoes and lightly kiss his lips. He smiles as I pull back, his eyes lighting with the desire for more.

"Let's go home." I say, and we climb into the truck and head back to where it all began.

Chapter Twenty-Nine

Ryan

I eye Sam out of my periphery as I guide us onto the interstate and head toward Hahira. She's been holding that folded sheet of paper since we left the rehab facility twenty minutes ago. She hasn't opened it, just passes it between her fingers in contemplation.

"What are you going to do with it?" I ask, pulling her attention to me. She worries at her lip and raises in the seat to tuck the paper back into her pocket.

"I don't know, to be honest. I'm not sure I'm ready to go potentially upend someone's life for my own benefit. Who knows what his life is like right now, and he doesn't even know I exist," Sam says, anxiety and fear riddling her words.

"And he won't know until someone tells him," I point out. There's a guy out there who was once in love with Annie and helped create Sam, yet he doesn't even know about her.

"What if I show up on his doorstep, and he turns me away? What if he's married, and my existence shatters the foundation of their relationship?" Sam asks, her voice shaking with emotion.

"Then the foundation of their relationship wasn't strong to begin with," I respond confidently. "And if he turns us away, then we will drive right over to Dot's where we know we'll be greeted with open arms." Sam smiles warmly at the mention Dot, and I continue. "But at least you will have given him the choice, and if he chooses not to know you, well then, that's his loss."

Sam sighs and shakes her head as she rubs her palms against her shorts in that way she always does when she's nervous.

"I'm just not sure I'm in the right head space right now to risk that sort of rejection again. I mean, I think sheer adrenaline and grief drove me to Annie's doorstep, and she always knew about me. I've barely processed the last week of my life. I think I need to get myself in a better place mentally and emotionally before I open myself up to any more trauma," she states with a sad smile, and my heart aches at her words. She's been through so much in such a short span of time. It makes complete sense that she may not be ready to add meeting her birth father to the list.

"Well, when you decide you're ready, I'll be right there with you," I say as check my side mirror and switch lanes. My eyes linger for a moment on the black car with tinted windows that's been behind us since leaving the main road of the rehab center. While I-75 is a major interstate that runs through multiple states, something about the vehicle sets my nerves on edge.

"You will be?" Sam asks, pulling me back to the conversation. I look at her and laugh lightly.

"Of course I will, Sam. I'll even drive," I say with a wink. Sam smiles, and she leans over the center console to kiss me softly on the cheek.

"Thank you for everything you've done, Ryan, and for always being there," Sam says softly before pulling back, and I glance over at her with a smile.

"Even when you didn't want me to be?" I ask and watch as Sam's smile brightens.

"Especially then." She says, and I grin like an idiot as I check the rearview mirror again to see the same black car still lingering behind us. Knowing that Josiah is still on the run makes me paranoid, and being on a three-hour stretch of interstate with the same vehicles behind us the whole time isn't putting me at ease.

"Have you heard from your mom at all?" Sam asks as I watch the black car swap lanes and fall a few cars behind. I let out a shaky breath and focus back on Sam.

"Uh, she's tried texting and calling a few times since we left, but I haven't answered. Honestly, I didn't tell her I was leaving to go with you because I didn't think she'd care," I admit. It didn't even cross my mind to tell her.

"Maybe she's calling because she cares," Sam says optimistically. I scoff and laugh a little.

"Not likely. She's probably wondering why I haven't been there to pick up all her empty beer bottles at night after she passes out on the couch. Waking up to the mess you've made rather than having it already cleaned for you is probably a tad inconvenient." Though I guess taking care of her over the last two years has been better than the alternative of being beaten by my dad every day. Mom used to not drink, but she'd still be just as absent as she hid in their bedroom while Dad raged on me downstairs.

"Do you think she's like Annie was? Self-medicating to help the pain and too far into it to see a way out?" Sam asks empathetically. My mind has also drawn the obvious parallels between my mom and Annie, but unlike my mom, Annie did what she thought would be best to protect her child. Even if that meant damning herself to a life of guilt and regret. All my mom has ever done is protect herself.

"I don't know," I answer honestly. "She holds down a steady job and seems to socialize decently. It's just at home that she feels the need to drink herself numb. Makes me wonder if maybe I'm the problem," I say with a shrug of my shoulders. The words hit my heart with a heavy weight, and I remember the haunted feeling I'd get as a child wondering what was so wrong with me that my dad would choose to treat me the way he did.

"It's not you, Ryan. Whatever demons she's fighting, they're hers. You didn't create them," Sam states strongly. The emotion in her tone makes me glance over at her. Tears fill her eyes as she scans my face, and she shakes her head.

"I'm so sorry for how I've treated you all these years. You were just a kid needing a safe place to land, and I went out of my way to make a bad situation worse," Sam says as a tear slides down her cheek. I glance at the road and then reach out to wipe at the tear.

"Hey, you didn't know that it was a bad situation. To you, I was just the annoying boy next door who wouldn't leave you alone. So, basically exactly who I am today." I smile as I focus back on the road and check the rearview mirror again. I don't see the black car this time and breathe a sigh of relief.

"Promise to never change then?" She says as she laughs and wipes her cheeks.

"I promise," I tell her. Sam smiles and goes back to looking out the window as I ponder what type of situation I'll be walking into with my mom. These last few days with Sam, Dot, and Annie, have really cemented my desire for that family bond that I used to get from Mark and Rose. I want the family dinners, movie nights, holidays spent making cookies and decorating. That's never been my family, and I'm not sure my mom has it in her to give me that.

Chapter Thirty

Sam

Sometime later, we pull into my driveway, and Ryan checks the rearview mirror for the hundredth time. He did that a lot on the drive down, though every time I looked in the mirror, I couldn't pinpoint what he was looking for.

"What's wrong?" I ask, concerned with the anxious shift in his usually relaxed demeanor. He looks around the empty street and shakes his head.

"Nothing, I've just had a weird feeling since we left the rehab center. I don't know, I think the fact that Josiah's still out there is getting to me," Ryan says, a dark look in his eyes as he glances down at the cast on my arm.

I unbuckle and reach across, placing my uninjured hand on his leg.

"Hey, they'll find him. It's just a matter of when. We're home now, and we don't have to worry about him anymore. The cops are keeping an eye on Dot's place, and if he tries anything, they'll be there. We're good, Ryan," I say, and I can feel him relaxing slightly under my touch.

"You're right," Ryan states, leaning over to capture my lips against his. It's quick, sweet, and feels completely normal, like it's something we've been doing our whole lives. "Let's get you inside," he says as he pulls back and opens the truck door.

We unload the truck and quickly settle into the quiet house. It feels odd to be back here after such a short amount of time filled with so much grief and discovery. The girl that I was that morning of graduation feels like a distant memory; she was cruel to herself and everyone around her. She's not someone I want to be again, though I know that she will always be a part of me.

"I'm going to start seeing a therapist," I say to Ryan as I hand him a fresh mug of coffee. We settle onto the couch together, The Office reruns playing on the tv. Ryan glances at me as he sips the steaming coffee and smiles. The warmth in his smile settles over me like sunshine.

"I'm proud of you, Sam," he says, placing his hand on the inside of my thigh, his thumb caressing my scars. I never thought that I would let someone see that part of me, to admit that I've battled and lost to my demons more times than I can count. Yet, Ryan has a way of making me feel like even the worst parts of myself are worth seeing and loving.

I set my coffee down and grab his mug out of his hand, setting it on the coffee table as well.

"Hey, I—," he begins, but I cut off his words as I crash my mouth against his. He falls back onto the cushion, my weight falling on top of him. His mouth parts immediately, and our tongues meet in a desperate dance of desire. Ryan moans, and the sound feeds the pressure building in my core.

His hands slide under my shirt, his fingers gliding up and down my back. Goosebumps erupt along my flesh, and I press my hips into his, desperate for friction. His cock grows thicker beneath me, and I moan into his mouth.

"Fuck, Sam," he breathes against my lips, and then he's yanking my shirt over my head and ripping his own off. We work in tandem to remove our clothes, and Ryan rolls a condom on before I position myself over his hips again.

I press my casted hand to his chest and wrap the other around the base of his cock. He groans, and his cock twitches under my touch. I position the tip at my center and glide it through my wet folds teasing us both. Ryan's hands grip my hips trying to bring me down onto his shaft, but I hold steady, circling the tip.

"Nah uh," I tease. "Not until you make me cum," I state seductively, and Ryan's eyes blaze with explosive heat. His thumb finds my clit, and he circles it as I continue to glide him through my center. His other hand grasps my breast in a painfully pleasurable hold, tweaking my nipple as he pinches my clit. The pressure inside of me reaches a crescendo, and I cry out as Ryan pinches my clit again. The waves of my orgasm rack my body as I slide down onto his hard cock.

"Fuck," Ryan mutters, releasing my breast to place both of his hands on my hips. His grip is bruising, and I relish the feeling of his fingers pressing into my curves. I slowly sink lower onto him, letting my body adjust to his size until I'm taking him completely. I gasp as Ryan uses his grip on my hips to move me up and down, angling his hips to thrust deeper into me. The angle has me throwing my head back and crying out, my body vibrating with rapidly building pleasure.

I move up and down in an intoxicating rhythm and lean forward to press my lips against Ryan's. His tongue swirls around mine as my walls clench around his cock. I break the kiss and pull back just enough to look into his beautiful grey-blue eyes. Emotion strangles me as I look at the person who has been here for every part of my life, seen every part of me, and still chooses to love me. My heart beats erratically as I slide up and down his cock.

"I'm falling in love with you, too," I breathe, and my heart stutters as his movements still. His eyes darken with intense longing and surprise.

"Say it again," Ryan demands, his grip tightening around my hips.

"I love you, Ryan," I say again, this time with a smile as the confidence builds inside of me. The words feel freeing, like letting go of a weight that has nearly drowned me for years. I've always felt so alone, caged by the darkness inside of me, but I'm finally choosing to step out of that cage and let myself love and be loved.

"I'll make it worth it, baby," Ryan says deeply, and then he's sitting up suddenly and shifting our bodies so that I now lay on the sofa as he thrusts into me. I scream his name as he hits that spot inside of me that has stars dancing in my vision. I come apart around him, my nails digging into his biceps, the muscles bulging beneath my touch. The aftershocks of my orgasm are unrelenting as Ryan thrust into me with a look of pure euphoria. He slams into me over and over until another orgasm rips through me just as he trembles above me, his cock twitching inside of me with release.

We stay there for a moment, just breathing and enjoying the comfort of our bodies being pressed against each other. Sometime later, we take a shower after Ryan wraps my cast with a grocery bag to keep it dry. I hold it above my head just to be safe as he gets on his knees in the shower and worships my body, making me come undone once again.

After the shower, we get dressed, and Ryan eyes my bed.

"Do you want to stay?" I ask, having already assumed that he would. I'm not sure how this works now that we are back home, and he has a perfectly good bed in his own home right next door.

"I do," Ryan begins. "Just let me run over to my house, check in with my mom, and grab a few things. I'll be back over shortly, okay?"

I nod and follow him downstairs, watching as he grabs his bags and heads for the door.

"I'll be back in a few minutes," Ryan says, leaning down to give me a gentle kiss.

"Hurry back," I whisper, not ready to be in this house alone for too long. Ryan's presence is like eternal sunshine keeping the darkness at bay. I'm not sure I can handle being without his light for long right now. He smiles and then leaves, shutting the door behind him.

I carry our nearly full mugs of cold coffee to the kitchen sink, laughing softly at the reminder of how I interrupted our coffee session. Just as I'm pouring the liquid down the sink, I hear the front door open and close again.

"Wow, that was fast," I say, setting the mugs in the sink and turning to walk into the living room. I round the corner with a smile and suddenly slam into a hard body. Rough hands grip my arms tightly, and the air leaves my lungs as I stare into a pair of dangerously dark eyes.

"I thought he'd never leave."

Chapter Thirty-One

Ryan

Hesitantly, I leave Sam's house and walk next door to my own. I don't like leaving her alone in the house her dad just died in last week. Though it feels like a lifetime has existed since I found them on his bedroom floor, I know it hasn't been long enough to even begin to process that trauma.

Walking into my house, I throw my keys on the kitchen counter and head into the living room. I expect my mother to be passed out on the sofa or at least halfway drunk by now. What I don't expect, however, is for her to come barreling through the living room and crashing into me.

"Ryan!" She cries as her arms wrap around my neck, and I stand frozen in utter shock for a moment before wrapping my arms around her waist. My brows crease with concern as she tightens our embrace.

"Mom, what happened?" I ask worriedly.

"What happened?!" Mom asks loudly as she pulls back to gape at me. "You left Ryan! I came home and you were gone. Your truck wasn't here, and your suitcase was missing. I thought you left me," she sobs, and my heart constricts. She doesn't look drunk at all. In fact, I don't see a single beer bottle anywhere in the living room.

"I'm sorry, Mom. I drove Sam to a town near Atlanta for a few days. There were some things there she needed to do after her dad passed. I honestly didn't think you'd notice," I admit, and her brows furrow in disbelief.

"You thought I wouldn't notice? Ryan, the second you didn't come home and didn't answer the phone, it felt like a hole had been blasted through my chest. I notice every second that you aren't here," she states passionately. Her words scratch at the irritation I've felt at her for the last two years, and I let it rise to the surface.

"You care so much about where I've been the last few days but not about anything I've done the last few years? Come on, Mom. You never came to a single football game or cared when I'd sneak out for a party. Hell, you didn't even come to my graduation," I say, finally clearing the air that has been fraught with tension for years.

"Because I didn't deserve to experience or know those things! I failed you for so many years, Ryan. The last thing I should have been able to experience was the proud moments of being your mother as if I've ever earned that title!" She cries, and rage bubbles over in me because that's the dumbest fucking thing I've ever heard.

"But punishing yourself was punishing me! How can you not see that?!" I yell, and her cheeks flush with shame.

"Ryan—" she starts, but I interrupt.

"You didn't stop Dad or protect me from him when he was here, and part of me understood that. You were scared of him, too. But after he left, you had the chance to do better, and you chose not to. You basically left me, too," I say, my voice cracking. Mom's eyes fill with tears, and she grabs my hands in hers and holds them tightly.

"I'm so sorry, Ryan. I should have said those words a long time ago. I thought if I could just work enough to keep a roof over our heads and food on the table, then I'd be doing enough, but I was wrong. You deserve more than just walls and a roof. You deserve to feel loved and safe, and when I thought you weren't coming back over these last few days, I thought I'd missed my chance to say those words," she says shakily as her hands grip mine tightly.

"I love you, Ryan. Please give me the chance to do better now. I'll be better, I promise. Just please give me a chance," she sobs with a desperate energy, and I drop our hands to yank her into my arms. She sobs against my chest as I bend my neck to bury my face into her raven hair.

"I love you so much, Mom," I murmur against her shoulder. "I would never leave you," I promise. She hugs me tighter as the weight of our issues lightens around us.

"I'm so proud of you, baby, and I'm so sorry," she says as we pull apart. She sniffles and wipes at her puffy eyes. She looks worn with exhaustion and worry, and guilt tugs at my heart for not calling her back over these last few days.

"Now, tell me what's going on between you and Sam," my mother says with a pointed look. I can't help the smile that plays on my lips as I think of the girl next door. I move to the couch to sit, and my mom drops into the spot next to me.

"She's amazing, but life has thrown a lot of shit at her lately. She's experienced more trauma in the last week than some experience in their whole life. I'm just trying to be there for her and remind her of how strong she is," I explain to Mom. I'm certainly not going into the physical details of our relationship with my mother, but something about the grin she gives me tells me that she's already surmised as much.

"Does she know that you're in love with her?" She asks, and I smile widely as I remember the way Sam told me she was falling in love with me as she sank down onto my cock.

"Yeah, she knows," I tell Mom and watch as her eyes water again.

"You have such a pure heart, baby. Just don't let her break it, okay?" Mom says as she reaches over to pat my leg in a comforting gesture. Her words remind me of Sam and her utter fear of being loved. She thinks loving her is a curse, and I'm determined to prove her wrong.

"She's worth the risk, Mom," I state confidently, and Mom just sighs before standing.

"Well then, I suppose it's time I meet the girl who's worth my boy's heart, huh? Why don't you call her and see if she wants to come over for a movie? She shouldn't be all alone over there, and I'd like to get to know her." Excitement electrifies my veins as I imagine having a movie night with Sam and my mother.

"Really?" I ask in disbelief. Mom nods and heads for the kitchen.

"I'll put on some popcorn, and if she doesn't feel up to it, then you and I can just watch a movie," she states as she begins opening cabinets.

I grin wildly as I stand and grab my phone. It feels like I've stepped into some surreal dream that I never want to wake from. I press Sam's contact and hold the phone to my ear as it rings. I count each ring as I wait for the sound of her voice. It never comes though, and I'm greeted by the automated voicemail system.

I frown and hang up, contemplating calling again. I decide against it and walk into the kitchen where the smell of popcorn fills the air.

"She didn't answer, but I know she's not asleep yet. I'm just going to run over there real quick and get her. I won't be long," I tell my mom, and she turns to me with a soft smile.

"Okay, baby. I'll get us a movie ready," she says, and my heart squeezes as I look down at the trash can to see it filled with unopened bottles of beer. She really is trying to be the person that I've always needed her to be.

I propel myself forward and throw my arms around her. She staggers back a little with a small laugh before wrapping her arms around me.

"Thank you," I whisper before I pull back to kiss her cheek.

"Don't thank me, baby. It's what I should have done all along," she says with a sad smile. I nod and swallow past the lump in my throat. Man, this has been one hell of a night.

"I'll be right back," I tell her as I turn to head out the door. I sprint quickly across the lawn and approach the large tree by Sam's window. I could use the front door, of course, but where's the fun in that? I imagine her lying in bed already in her oversized t-shirt and tiny shorts just waiting for me to get back. That lustful surprised look that I know she'll give me fills my mind, and I laugh quietly as I begin climbing the large branches.

Chapter Thirty-Two

Sam

My heart stops as the sound of Josiah's deep voice sends ice through my veins. His grip is bruising above my elbows, and his unsettling grin is made darker by the still healing bruises around his eyes and nose from our last encounter.
"G—get out," I stutter, trying to push against his chest. He laughs and yanks me against him, his rancid breath beating down on me as he speaks.

"You and I have unfinished business," he growls, his greasy hair and stench a stark contrast to the meticulously put together man I met before. It's clear he hasn't showered in days, his wrinkled clothes a reminder of his time on the run.

"Did you follow us here?" I ask fearfully, remembering Ryan's nervous energy the entire drive home. He felt like someone had been following us, and he had been right. Josiah's nails dig into my skin, and I cry out. He smirks and leans into me, his lips ghosting over my ear.

"You owe me a lot of money, and I'm here to collect," Josiah shakes me roughly as he finishes speaking, and I open my mouth to scream Ryan's name. Only a squeak of surprise comes out, however, as Josiah tosses me into the living room. I stumble as I try to get my feet under me, but I fall forward, crashing into the coffee table. My forehead catches the corner of the wood as I tumble to the floor, and pain erupts in my skull.

I lay there dazed and moan as I lift my hand to wipe at the warm liquid sliding down my temple. My fingers come away red, and my stomach turns as my blood drips onto the hardwood floor.

"You see," Josiah says calmly as he takes a few steps toward me. "I've never been one for guns. I've always been more of a knife guy myself," he states, and my heart pounds in sync with my head as I push myself to my hands and knees. Josiah watches me with a violent glimmer in his eyes as he slowly pulls out a pocketknife and releases the large blade with a flick of his wrist.

"Had I known Annie liked to play with guns, I would have come more prepared for our last encounter. How's that old saying go?" Josiah asks, nonchalantly tapping the blade of his knife against his upper arm where the bullet grazed him at Annie's. "Don't bring a knife to a gunfight, right? Well, I say it's time we settle the score."

He advances on me just as I get to my feet, my vision blurring as blood drips into my right eye. His arm slashes out at me, and I swing my injured hand out, the hard cast crashing into his jaw. Josiah drops the knife with a grunt, the metal clattering to the floor.

"You fucking bitch," he seethes, and his hand flies out before I can move. His backhand slams into my left cheekbone, and the force of his swing knocks me to the side. I fall to my knees again, my head swimming and my vision blacking around the edges.

A thin trail of blood begins smearing across the hardwood as I start crawling toward the front door, desperate to escape. A sob leaves my throat as the sound of Josiah's footsteps grows louder. I try to get my footing under me and reach for the door with blood-soaked fingers. Just as my slick palm connects with the doorknob, a hand fists into my hair, yanking me back with violent force.

I scream as Josiah drags me by the hair across the floor, my chance of escape dwindling with each step.

"RYAN!" I scream with everything in me. Josiah throws me down next to the couch and drops down to straddle my hips. I open my mouth to scream again, but his hand clamps down over my mouth with bruising force.

"Shut the fuck up," he growls, pressing down on my mouth and silencing my sobs. Tears stream down my temples mixing with blood and sweat. I try to lash out with my fists, but Josiah just blocks the blows with his chest as he reaches over to grab his knife off the floor. I scream into his hand and begin thrashing under his weight, the balls of my feet slamming into the floor and my knees smacking against his back. He presses the knife to my throat, and my movements freeze.

"You and I are going to go for a little ride tonight, and in the morning, you're going to drain that pretty little bank account of yours. Then, I'm going to take you to Atlanta and collect on what's mine," Josiah snarls as he presses the blade closer to my skin. The metal bites into my neck, and a trickle of warm liquid glides down my skin.

"But first, I'm due my pound of flesh," Josiah states darkly, and I sob pleadingly against his hand. I thrash beneath him and choke on my own muffled screams as he readjusts his grip on the knife. The metal glints as he raises it into the air before bringing it down to slam into my shoulder. His fingers flex against my mouth as I scream, a burning pain erupting in my arm and chest. I spasm beneath him, my body fighting to escape the blade.

Josiah moans as he presses the blade deeper and twists it. A sick squelching noise permeates the air, and my eyes roll as dizziness overwhelms me.

"I love how intimate a blade can be. You just don't get that with a gun," he states as he drops his hand from my mouth to press against my chest. "See how I can feel your heart pumping the blood out of your body to coat my blade? It's unlike any other feeling," Josiah says right before he abruptly snatches the blade out of my shoulder.

A weak cry escapes me, and Josiah's weight disappears as he stands to watch my blood drip from the blade. He catches a drop on his finger and then brings it to his mouth.

"Mmm," he hums as the blood touches his tongue, and I cry out in disgust as I force my body to roll over.

"You're fucking crazy," I snarl as I try to push myself up to stand. There's no way I'm leaving here with this psycho. He'll have to kill me first. Josiah just laughs as he steps closer to me.

"I'll never give you a dime, and the cops are already all over your friend in Atlanta," I lie, strapping on my best poker face. "They'll arrest you the second you get there." Josiah's grin wavers slightly, and his hand flexes around the handle of the blade. I finally get my legs to cooperate and stand as I press my hand into my bleeding shoulder.

"What the fuck did the police tell you?" Josiah spits, and I take the opening to place more doubt in his mind. Maybe if I can convince him that this idiotic plan of his won't work, then self-preservation will win out, and he'll fucking run and leave me the hell alone.

"Enough to know that if you don't go hide in a hole for the rest of your days, then you're fucking done." Josiah's whole demeanor changes at my words, and I realize then that I've forgotten one other option that he has.

It's not just between taking me to Atlanta and running or leaving me here and fleeing. He could also choose to just kill me and disappear. Josiah's eyes glint as he seems to be making that same deduction. He grins as he flips the knife in his hand.

"Well then, I suppose I better make that pound of flesh worth it," he states. Before I can process his words, Josiah charges at me. I scream and bolt for the front door again. My bloody hand grips the handle and snatches the door open just as Josiah closes in. I take one step onto the porch when his hand grabs my hair and yanks me back inside, shattering my hopes of escaping.

My back slams against the wall as Josiah presses into me, kicking the door shut.

"You should have just left well enough alone." The words are barely out of his mouth when a searing pain slices across my side and through my stomach. I try to scream, but nothing comes out as Josiah pulls his blade out of my abdomen and lets me slide down the wall.

I press my casted hand to the wound as blood pulses out of my body. Pain like I've never experienced envelops every part of me, and I sob as I let go of the wound to try and crawl away from him.

Josiah laughs as I slowly drag myself across the floor, my body quickly becoming numb to the pain and my vision darkening further. My phone lays by the coffee table, having been knocked off earlier, and I reach for it with a bloody hand. A ringing sound fills the air as my phone lights up, and Ryan's beautiful face fills the screen.

I sob as I desperately try to grab the phone. My fingernails break against the hardwood floor as I claw my way toward it. I spent so much of my life wanting the abyss to swallow me whole, but in this moment, I'm fighting with everything in me to not let the darkness pull me under. I do not want to die, not here and not now.

I want to live long enough to be wrapped in Dot's arms again, see Annie leave rehab, and watch Ryan's first college game. This is not how it ends for me. Death can go fuck itself today.

With one last reach, I grasp the phone just as the screen goes black. I scream in frustration as Josiah laughs again, the sound closer this time. Just as I'm about to unlock my phone, Josiah's boot comes down on the screen, knocking it from my hand. He kicks it away, and I cry out as I try to push myself up onto my hands and knees.

"Stay down, little daisy. It'll all be over soon," Josiah says, and I shake my head to fight against the pull of unconsciousness.

"Fuck you," I snarl as I push myself up to my feet, dizziness threatening to topple me back over. Josiah throws his head back and laughs, and the sound fuels my rage.

"We can work that out if you think you'll last another twenty minutes," he states casually as he tilts his head to eye me appreciatively. My stomach rolls at the thought.

"Over my dead body," I snarl, and Josiah laughs as if this is all just a joke.

His laughter is cut short, though, when I slam my casted hand into his crotch with such force that it feels as if I'm breaking the bone all over again. As Josiah cries out and doubles over, I pull my hand back to slam it into his face. The strike knocks him off balance, sending him crashing to the floor.

With everything left in me, I stumble toward the front door. My vision darkens as the steady stream of blood paints my clothes and hands. I grab the knob and try to turn it, but an icy cold settles into my bones as everything goes numb. I hear a distant thud and a scream, and then I'm suddenly falling as the darkness finally pulls me under.

Chapter Thirty-Three

Ryan

The moment my leg is over the windowsill of Sam's room, my smile disappears as terror floods my veins. The sounds of a violent struggle pierce my ears, and a protective rage catapults me through the room and into the hall. A masculine roar of pain reverberates through the house, and panic electrifies me when I don't hear a sound from Sam. It's Josiah, it must be. He followed us here, and I fucking left her here alone. I'm going to fucking kill him.

Ripping out my phone and rushing across the hall to Mark's room, I dial 9-1-1.

"9-1-1, where is your emergency?" The operator greets, and my heart pounds in my chest as I grab the baseball bat from Mark's room and ease back into the hall.

"115 Crest Hill Drive. There's an intruder. Get here now," I growl and slide the phone into my pocket, leaving the line open. I rush down the stairs with my heartbeat pounding in my ears and freeze at the base of the stairs. Blood streaks the hardwood floor, and Sam's phone lays shattered in the corner. My vision blurs with panic as I spot Sam stumbling to the front door, Josiah rushing at her from behind.

My grip tightens painfully on the bat as I run forward. Sam's hand just grazes the doorknob as Josiah reaches for her hair. I roar as I swing the bat with all my strength. The wood cracks against Josiah's skull with a resounding thud, and blood sprays across the already streaked wall. The vibration of the impact rattles through my bones. Josiah drops to the floor in an unconscious heap just as Sam tries to turn the knob. She sways on her feet, and then she's falling.

I drop the bat and catch her in my arms as she drops, blood instantly coating my hands. Warm red liquid covers the entire left side of her upper body and trickles down her head from an open wound. Her eyelids flutter as she goes slack in my arms, and I press my fingers into her neck desperate to feel the thump of her pulse. It's thready under my touch, and I lay her flat on the floor to assess the extent of her wounds.

There's a stab wound to her shoulder, but the worst of the blood seeps from a gash in her abdomen.

"Stay with me, Sam. Stay with me," I plead as I move to grab a throw blanket off the nearby sofa. I step over Josiah's prone form to drop back down next to Sam and press the balled-up blanket against her abdomen. She moans against the pain, and I reach a blood-stained hand out to cup her cheek.

"Come on, baby. Keep your eyes open," I beg as tears fill my eyes. I press harder against the wound as more blood seeps from her shoulder and head wounds. There's so much blood, and I can't do enough to stop it. Her eyes flutter again, and those bright blue eyes meet mine for just a moment.

"Ryan," Sam whispers with a pale smile. Her voice is weak as her eyes start to close again, and I snap my fingers in front of her face.

"Hey! Eyes on me, Sam! Come on, baby, look at me," I command, trying to keep her from falling unconscious. Sirens sound outside as the yellow blanket I'm pressing against her stomach becomes stained red.

"I don't want to die, Ryan," Sam mutters softly, her eyes glazed and unfocused. My heart stops beating at her words, and my cheeks become wet as my muscles strain under the tension of the pressure I'm applying. I press harder against her wound, and I'm terrified that I'm hurting her.

"You're not going to die, Sam," I growl with intensity as the sirens grow closer. How fucking slow are they going? Josiah moans from a few feet away, and I swear if he tries to get up, I'm going to cave his head in with that bat.

"I fought, I promise," Sam whispers as I hear shouts and slamming coming from outside.

"And you're not done fighting, do you hear me?" I lean down and brush some of her blood-matted hair away from her temple, and my stomach turns at the amount of red that covers her body.

Sam groans as the paleness in her face spreads to her lips, and a loud banging shakes the front door.

"Fight harder, Samamtha," I snap as her warm blood soaks through the blanket, and her eyes droop closed. There is no fucking way I'm losing her.

"HPD, we're coming in! Keep your hands where we can see them!" Shouts echo through the room as the front door flies open, and multiple uniformed officers storm in with their guns trained on me.

"Hands up!" One of the officers yells as his gun sweeps the area before landing back on me.

"Unless you're coming to put pressure on this wound, my hands aren't moving. I'm the one who called you," I try to state calmly as Sam's life bleeds away beneath my touch.

"All clear," Another one says as he cuffs a groaning Josiah's hands behind his back.

"Medics come in, it's all clear," the officer says into his radio as he lowers his gun. "We have one suspect with a head wound and a young female with multiple stab wounds." I grit my teeth at his words and try to tap Sam's cheek with one hand while keeping pressure with the other. She doesn't stir, and dizzying fear blurs my vision.

"Come on, Sam," I plead as a medic drops down next to me. I hold my breath as he presses his fingers against her neck.

"I've got a pulse. Sir, I need you to let go now and let me treat her," he says, and my body starts to shake with relief. She's still here, she's still fighting. Reluctantly, I allow the officer to pull me up as the medic slides into my place and starts packing bandages against Sam's wounds. Another medic steps in with a stretcher and begins applying a blood pressure cuff and oxygen.

I step back as they load her onto the stretcher and watch as an officer pulls a cuffed and moaning Josiah off the floor. His eyes track the movements of the medics as they frantically bandage Sam and start to move her to the ambulance. A sick grin splits his face as his gaze turns to meet mine.

"Guess I got my pound of flesh," he states with bravado, and I lunge at him, my arm swinging back. The officer next to me catches my fist midair, and I whirl on him with rage burning through me.

"I wouldn't do that if I were you. I don't want to have to arrest you for assault," he states calmly. Josiah laughs as the officers guide him outside and to another ambulance. I shake off the officer without responding as I rush out the door just as Sam is being loaded into the ambulance. Red and blue lights fill the night sky, bleeding into the pearlescent glow of the full moon above.

"Ryan!" My mother yells as she comes running across our yard. She collides into my chest, and I wrap my arms around her in a strong embrace.

"Mom," I choke, and I almost lose it. A medic shouts at me, and I pull back from my mother's arms.

"I have to go," I say brokenly as I turn to run toward the shutting ambulance doors.

"Go! I'll be right behind you," My mom shouts as I climb into the back of the ambulance and fall into a seat next to the stretcher. The doors shut, and the ambulance takes off with the sirens blaring. The medic in the back with me packs more bandaging on Sam's wounds and radios to the hospital to prepare a blood transfusion.

My eyes zero in on her face as I hold her rapidly chilling hand in mine.

"Come on, baby. Keep fighting," I plead as the ambulance barrels through an intersection. The monitor above us beeps and then begins to blare in warning.

"She's bottoming out!" The medic shouts as he pushes me out of the way. My heart stops as the blaring beeps turn into a monotone flatline.

"Starting compressions!" The medic shouts to the driver as he positions himself over Sam and begins pressing into her chest with terrifying force. Sam's body jostles under the rapid movements, her blood-stained hands hanging limply over the sides of the stretcher.

Bile rises in my throat as I grip the edge of my seat. The sirens become a distant sound as my pulse pounds in my head, while hers is nowhere to be found.

She's dying. This can't be happening. The medic's face is red with fatigue as he presses into her chest over and over. His eyes glance from me to the monitor and back down to Sam.

"Do not stop," I snarl at him as I lean forward to grip Sam's lifeless hand. Death holds her in its unforgiving clutches, but I'm not letting it have her.

"You have to fight, Sam. Fight!"

Chapter Thirty-Four

Ryan

Two weeks later, the gravel under my feet gives way to grass as I approach the row of sunlit headstones. Small patches of weeds peek through the dirt of the freshest grave, and the bouquet of tulips and daisies in my hand crinkle in the warm June wind.

Grief weighs heavy on my heart as I stare at the engraving on the headstone in front of me and the temporary placard sitting on the grave next to it. I sigh as I bend down and place the daisies and tulips in front of the headstone and step back.

"I really miss them," Sam says as her hand grabs mine, her fingers threading through my own. I grip her hand tightly as I look back down at Rose and Mark's grave.

"I do, too," I state solemnly. What I don't say, however, is how thankful I am that there isn't a third grave here. I thought I knew fear as a child when my father would let his monster rage, but that night two weeks ago was a whole new level of terror that I never want to experience again.

Sam died. For a whole six minutes, Samantha Grace Miller was dead. I screamed at the medic to keep doing CPR and pleaded with everything in me for her to come back, to fight to live. Once the ambulance lurched to a halt, nurses and doctors pulled the stretcher out and took over the medic's compressions.

I stumbled out of the ambulance behind them as a nurse ripped Sam's shirt off and started attaching pads and wires to her chest.

"Clear!" Someone yelled as everyone stepped back from the stretcher, and Sam's body jolted with shock. A single beep filled the air, and I nearly fell to my knees as the weak pulse returned to Sam's heart.

They rushed her to surgery where she spent the next four hours receiving blood as the doctors repaired the damage Josiah's blade had caused. My mother sat next to me in the waiting room as I stared at my bloodstained hands. I couldn't bring myself to wash them until I was certain that Sam would come back to me, that the blood on my hands wouldn't be all that remained of her.

Hours later, my soul returned to my body as Sam's eyes fluttered open again.

"Ryan," she sobbed as her gaze met mine, and I cradled her face in my hands as I pressed my lips to hers. I savored the sound of the surprised breath she released and the warmth of her skin as she kissed me back.

She's alive. After everything, she defied death and fought like hell to come back. She sobbed on the phone with Dot as she laid in the hospital bed, assuring her grandmother that she was okay and begging her not to tell Annie about the attack. Sam didn't want to chance compromising her recovery and told Dot that she would tell Annie everything she needed to know when the time was right.

My mother stayed by our side the whole time, bringing Sam and I changes of clothes and food. She even surprised Sam with her favorite iced hazelnut latte on her third day in the hospital. Sam had to stay in the hospital for a few days, and she spent the time making me sit as still as a statue as she sketched a portrait of me.

Now, she stands next to me with her casted arm in a sling and a healing scar on her forehead. Her power and strength are mesmerizing as I watch her bend down to place her own flowers on her father's grave.

"They would be so proud of you," I tell her, and she turns to stare at me with tear-filled eyes.

"That's all I ever wanted," she whispers, and I step forward to wrap my arms around her. I cradle her head against my chest and kiss her hair, the smell of coconuts and honey filling my senses.

"They were always proud," I say confidently, though I know Sam has spent years thinking the opposite. She just nods into my chest before pulling back to look up at me. A small smile plays on her lips as she reaches into her purse and retrieves an envelope. She holds it out to me, and confusion creases my brows.

"What's this?" I ask as I reach into the envelope and pull out the folded sheet of paper.

"I found it while looking through some of my parents' things yesterday. It belongs to you," she states with a glimmer in her eyes. I unfold the paper and freeze at the sight of the words on the sheet.

"This is the title to my truck," I say in confused disbelief. It's not just the title to the truck that has my heartbeat stuttering; it's Mark and Rose's names on the title that do, too.

"It was never your father that bought you the truck. It was my parents. My dad paid it off last year, and he had Dave transfer the title and insurance into your name when you turned eighteen. He's been paying the insurance every month," Sam says with a sad smile. A lump lodges itself in my throat as I think of the morning that I woke up on my sixteenth birthday to see the black truck in the drive with a bow on the hood.

I was shocked as I walked out there barefoot and bruised from my father's outburst the night before and couldn't believe that he would have gotten me a truck. I opened the driver's door to find a set of keys sitting on the leather and a note that said, 'happy birthday, Ryan'.

Hours later, when my father came storming into my room screaming about the truck outside, I assumed my mother had bought it. She said nothing, though, as she stayed locked in her room while I suffered at my father's hand. Just a week later, everything went down, and my father left. The truck stayed, and I never said anything to my mom about it.

I never thought for a second that it was a gift from Mark and Rose. Now, tears cloud my vision as the words on the page blur. I blink away the tears and look back to Sam's soft smile and wet eyes.

"You're not mad?" I ask hesitantly. I know Sam has always struggled with the relationship that I had with her parents, and this revelation is a glaring reminder of that. Sam just smiles wider and shakes her head.

"Who could be angry at someone for loving you?" She says as she lifts her uninjured hand to caress my cheek. I lean down and capture her lips with mine, savoring the taste of her. The salty taste of tears mingles with our kiss, and I pull back to wipe Sam's cheeks.

"I love you," I state as I hold her delicate face in my hands. Her beautiful blue eyes shimmer as she licks her plump lips, the lips that I plan to spend the rest of my life kissing.

"I love you, too," she says with a grin, and I pull her back into my arms as we stand there visiting her parents for a while longer.

"When do you leave for UGA?" Sam asks later as we walk back to the truck.

"Next week," I say as I help her into the truck and buckle her in. I have no idea what our relationship is going to look like once school starts, and I'm in Athens while she's here.

"Mind if I catch a ride with you? Considering I can't really drive myself right now," Sam says with a mischievous grin. My eyes widen in shocked confusion as I stare at her.

"Wh—what are you saying?" I stammer, trying not to get too excited in case I'm interpreting this all wrong.

"I got in," Sam explains, and my heart explodes with pride and joy. "I took your advice and reached out to the art department's director while I was in the hospital. You were right. I needed to show them who I truly am and not just who I thought they wanted to see."

"I'm so fucking proud of you," I declare as I grab her face and press my lips against hers. She smiles into the kiss, and euphoria floods my system. We pull apart, and I shut her door with a grin before walking around the truck to get into the driver's seat.

"So, what are you going to do with the house?" I ask, and Sam sighs with a shake of her head.

"I'm not ready to let it go. It's my parents' home and the biggest piece of them that I have left. I talked to Dave yesterday, and he's putting me in contact with a local property manager to help me rent it out. I'll just have to pack everything up and move it to storage until I'm ready to either move back into it or let it go." She smiles sadly at the thought, and I reach over to place my hand on her thigh as I drive us back to her house.

"At least renting it out will provide me with additional income while I'm away at college," Sam states, and I grin at the reminder that she's going to be right there with me.

"Any chance we end up being neighbors in Athens?" I ask jokingly, and Sam laughs lightly.

"Not a chance," she responds, and I shrug my shoulders.

"I guess I'll just have to wait until you're ready to move in with me to hear you moaning over your coffee every morning," I say with a wink, and Sam's cheeks flush with shock. I laugh at her wide-eyed stare as I turn us onto another road.

"Don't worry, baby, I know we have a long way to go. There's no rush, and when you decide you're ready, I'll be right here," I state as I caress her thigh in soothing strokes. Her hand lands on top of mine as she grips it tightly.

"You always are," she says with that beautiful smile that I know I'll spend the rest of my life trying to see.

Chapter Thirty-Five

Sam

Six Months Later...

Christmas used to be my least favorite holiday. The colorful lights and merriness of the season were typically a blinding contrast to the darkness I'd usually feel lingering inside of me. This year, however, I've spent the months leading up to Christmas talking to a therapist and diminishing the darkness one day at a time.

There are still moments where the darkness lingers, and the grief feels insurmountable. On those days, I lean away from the abyss rather than into it and fall into Ryan's arms. We'll spend hours snuggling in bed eating popcorn and watching comedy shows until I start to feel the darkness recede.

His presence in my life over the last six months has been unwavering, and I fall more in love with him every single day. He isn't afraid to ask me the hard questions, to see the look in my eyes when I leave a rough therapy session and confront it head on.

On the nights when the memory of our trauma haunts his eyes,

Ryan will mark my scars with his kiss, counting them one by one. We're able to find comfort in each other's presence, and I'm grateful every day that I got into UGA. I don't think either of us would have fared as well in the aftermath of Josiah's damage if we had been living hours apart.

Dot's house is only an hour from my apartment now, and I've spent many weekends in the warmth of her home being fed an abundance of homecooked meals and sweets. Annie's been working for the past few months as an Arts and Crafts Director at the local community center and loves it. She still lives with Dot, though she's been talking recently about getting her own apartment.

Tonight, however, we are all gathered in the living room sipping cocoa and watching The Grinch. The Christmas tree is shimmering with ornaments, lights, and tinsel, and presents line the floor around it. Ryan snuggles in closer to me, his hand on my thigh under the blanket. I lean into his touch, resting my head on his shoulder and savoring his warmth. He smells like the cologne I gave him for his birthday, the notes of sandalwood and citrus enveloping my senses.

"Okay, time for gifts! I can't hold back any longer," Annie says as she jumps up from the sofa. Ryan and I sit up as Dot smiles broadly from her recliner. Annie reaches under the tree and pulls out a small box, handing it to Dot. She grins as she points Annie to the large box wrapped in Elvis Presley paper.

"That one's yours, dear," Dot says, and Annie's eyes widen as she takes in the size of the box. One thing I've learned about Dot is how obsessed she is with anything Elvis Presley related. Annie, on the other hand, is more of an Eminem fanatic. While mother and daughter, they are two comically different people.

I watch with intrigue as Dot unwraps the small box from Annie, and gasps at its contents.

"Oh, honey," Dot whispers as she pulls a gold necklace from the box, the beautiful charm dangling in the air. A single daisy hangs from the necklace, tiny diamonds filling the petals. My eyes water as Dot brings a shaky hand to her mouth attempting to contain her sob.

"Annie, you didn't need to do this. You work so hard for your money, baby," Dot says, and Annie shakes her head.

"You deserve the world, Mama," Annie states as she leans down to press a kiss to Dot's forehead. She gently grabs the necklace from her mother's hands and clasps it around Dot's neck. The daisy pendant sits beautifully against her chest, and tears roll down Dot's face.

"I love it, Annie baby. Thank you," Dot says as Annie leans down to give her a hug. When Annie stands back up, Dot shoos her over to the large box waiting next to the tree. Annie looks nervous as her eyes meet mine, and I nod my head and give her an encouraging smile. I've also learned over the past few months, that Annie doesn't do well with receiving things, whether it be compliments, money, or gifts. She never feels as if she's deserving of whatever we try to give her, but her therapy has been helping some with that recently.

Annie unwraps the large box and shouts in glee as she takes in the sets of luxury canvases, paints, and brushes.

"Mama!" Annie exclaims as she turns and rushes to Dot, colliding with the recliner and throwing her arms around her mother. Dot just laughs and returns the embrace, whispering into Annie's ear and kissing her cheek. The sight makes my heart ache for the mother I grew up with, the one who would kiss my scraped knees and take me to the art supply store as many times as I wanted.

Therapy is helping me learn to cherish the memories I had with my parents while also trying to make new memories with the family I have here now. There are some days, though, when I'm weighed down with guilt at the idea that my parents would feel as if they're being replaced. Dot and Annie could never take their place or negate the memories I have of them, but I also don't want to waste any more time limiting and sacrificing the relationships around me because of my own doubts and fears.

Annie pulls my attention back to the exchange of gifts as she brings a large, thin rectangle over for me to unwrap.

"Oh, you didn't—" I start to say she didn't need to get me anything, but she just waves her hand in the air and presses the gift into my hands. Ryan moves in closer to me to watch as I pull the red and green paper off. My throat clogs with emotion as I take in the large canvas painting.

It's a gorgeous garden of daisies, roses, and tulips with bits of lavender popping up between the flowers. The array of bright colors and elegant brushstrokes showcase Annie's talent and passion.

"It's beautiful," I breathe as I find myself at a loss for words. It's more than just beautiful; it looks heavenly, as if you could step into it and smell the roses and caress the soft petals of the daisies. A single tree is painted on the outskirts of the garden with a swing hanging from it, a perfect symbol of innocence and childhood.

"I wanted to make something that could honor both sides of who you are and just how beautiful each part makes you," Annie says nervously, and tears flood my eyes, slipping down my cheeks in quick secession. I sit the painting in Ryan's lap and jump up to throw my arms around Annie.

"It's perfect," I cry into her shoulder, hugging her tightly. She breathes a sigh of relief over my shoulder, as if afraid I wouldn't like it. I pull away and wipe my eyes before reaching under the tree to hand her the gift I brought.

"It's not... much," I say, suddenly anxious. Annie gives me a look that tells me she doesn't care what it is, and my nerves ease slightly. She carefully peels off the paper and her mouth falls open in shock.

"Oh, Sam," She gasps, dropping the paper to the floor and

grasping the frame in her hands. She stares at it in disbelief for a long moment before turning it around to show Dot. My grandmother presses a hand to her heart, and tears brim her eyes.

"That's beautiful, little daisy," Dot says, and Annie turns the frame back around to hug it against her chest.

"I love it so much," she states as she walks over to the end table and sets the frame on it. A sketched photo of a young woman holding a baby wrapped in a daisy printed blanket stares back at me; an exact replica of the polaroid from eighteen years ago.

Annie's arms wrap around me suddenly, and I smile into her embrace.

"Merry Christmas," I whisper to her before pulling back and walking over to hand my grandmother her gift.

"Merry Christmas, Maw Maw," I tell her as I place the gift in her hands. She smiles softly at me as she tears into the paper and gasps.

"Samantha Grace Miller, you did not!" Dot exclaims, and I laugh as she jumps up and pulls me against her chest. My laughter spreads as Ryan catches sight of the gift and starts laughing as well. Annie steps forward and pulls the frame from Dot's hands.

"Oh, that's perfect," Annie says with a giggle as she holds up the Elvis Presley portrait that I sketched for days. Dot grabs it back from her and walks it over to place it right next to the polaroid sketch. An overwhelming sense of pride fills me, and Ryan walks over to wrap his arms around me and kiss the top of my head.

"You did good, babe," he says as he reaches down and grabs a gift bag from under the tree. He passes it to me, and I eye him with an inquisitive look. An arrogant grin fills his face as I reach into the bag to pull out the tissue paper. I reach the bottom of the bag, and my fingers touch a soft fabric.

I grasp it and pull it out, my mouth falling open. My heart stutters as I unfurl the shirt to see an exact replica of the Grumpy

Care-Bear shirt my dad had bought me for my birthday. That shirt had been used to stop Annie's bleeding and save her life, but I mourned it all the same. It was my most prized possession after his passing, and Ryan found a way to replace it.

"I love you," I say as I push up on my tiptoes to bring my lips to his. He smiles into the kiss before pulling back.

"I love you, too." He smiles as I hug the shirt to my chest, completely enamored by the man in front of me. God, I want to wake up every morning to that seductive smile and spend every night threading my fingers through his hair.

"Okay," I say suddenly, trying to hype myself up to give Ryan his present. His brows crease as I grab the tiny box and hand it to him. He eyes me for a moment, Dot and Annie looking at us with anticipation.

"You're not proposing to me, are you, Samantha?" Ryan jokes, and I laugh and roll my eyes.

"It's a proposal of sorts," I state as he finally unwraps the bow and opens the lid of the box. His eyes light with passion as he pulls the small gold key out attached to a UGA football keychain. He holds it up, and steps closer to me.

"Is this what I think it is, Samantha?" He asks with a knowing grin.

"Someone's gotta get you out of that awful frat house," I say, and Ryan laughs.

"It's not that bad," he responds, and I reach for the key.

"Then, I guess you won't be needing that," I say as I try to grab the key. He yanks it out of my reach, holding it as high as he can.

"Absolutely not, baby. You're never getting rid of me now," Ryan states, and Dot and Annie clap with shouts of excitement as he leans down to capture my lips in a celebratory kiss.

The next day, Ryan and I head home, and anticipation floods my veins at the thought of him moving in. He's my safe space, my confidante, my best friend, and my home.

"I've been thinking," I begin as I reach into my purse and pull out the small piece of folded paper.

"Oh yeah, about what?" Ryan says, glancing at me from the driver's seat.

"How do you feel about taking a road trip for spring break?" I ask as I begin to unfold the paper.

"A road trip with you? Sounds like a dream I once had. Where are we going?" Ryan asks with a wide smile.

I let out a breath as I look for the first time at the words on the paper that have been in my possession for months now. My heart stutters at the information written in Annie's handwriting. I can do this; it's time.

"To Washington," I state with a shaky voice. "It's time to meet my father."

Acknowledgement

There aren't enough words to quanitfy how much this book means to me and the people around me. Sam's story has lived in my mind for over ten years. She was born in some of my darkest days and became an embodiment of my thoughts and struggles. I've tried to write other stories over the years, but I would always find my way right back to Sam and Ryan. I could never get them out of my head but also wasn't mentally in a place where I could put their story on paper and see it through. That all changed this year, and I finally get to share the beautiful complexities of Sam and Ryan with you.

Firstly, I want to say thank you to my husband and the love of my life. Will, you are the Ryan to my Sam, my guiding light in the darkest days. Your heart and humor came barreling into my life thirteen years ago, and you've spent every day since showing me the true definition of love and safety. Thank you for listening to all of my midnight babblings about Sam and Ryan and for holding down the fort when I was too consumed with this book to do basic things like laundry and dishes. You are my hero and best friend, I love you so much.

To my Archer and Isabelle who won't be able to read this book until they're much older, you two are my lifeline. Thirty percent of this novel was typed with one hand while the other held your energetic toddler selves. Thank you both for teaching me what it means to love unconditionally and to be loved without the expectation of perfection. Being your mother has healed the child in me and given me the strength to finally tell this story. I love you both to the moon and back.

Thank you to my sisters, Bethany and Danielle, for being my beta readers and editors throughout this process. Bethany, thank you for reading this book chapter by chapter as I would write it even though you had a thousand other things to do. You've always made time for my hopes and dreams, and if there's one person I always knew believed in me, it's you. Danielle, you were the first one to finish this book, reading the last few chapters right after I sent them to you at midnight. Your unwavering enthusiasm for this story has carried me through this process. Sam's story is not just mine to tell, it's also both of yours. I love you both so much.

To my precious in-laws and my grandmother, you have showed me over the years how to be a selfless and loving parent, someone who is a safe space of kindness and comfort. I love you all so much, though you will be getting a family-friendly copy of this book with the spicy scenes blacked out (sorry).

To my Maw Maw Dot, I wish more than anything that you were here to see this novel come to fruition. For years, I would tell you of my hopes and dreams of being a writer, and you'd always say that you couldn't wait to see my name on the cover of a book one day. Well, I hope you can see this wherever you are, and I hope I made you proud. I miss you so damn much and would give anything to feel the warmth of your hugs again. I love you.

I'm so incredibly thankful to my family and friends for supporting me through this process and encouraging me every step of the way. I hope that Sam and Ryan's story helps anyone out there struggling with the darkness know that they are not alone. If you are dealing with depression or thoughts of self-harm, please reach out to your local resources and let them help guide you to safety. There is hope and light to be found; you matter, and the world is so much more beautiful with you in it.

Thank you to anyone that reads this book, and if you've made it this far into the acknowledgements, then you deserve a gold medal. And finally, to coffee and my nespresso machine, you fueled all the midnight writing sessions and saw me through the end.

Thank you a thousand times over for giving Sam and Ryan's story a chance. Stay tuned for the next chapter of their journey.

With love,
Bri

Made in the USA
Columbia, SC
06 October 2024